THE BATTLES OF
...N K...
COVENTRY

ONE WILL COME TO LEAD THE FIGHT, TO DEFEAT THE
DARKNESS, BRING THE TRIUMPH OF THE LIGHT.

ONE WILL COME WITH FIRE AS HIS CROWN,

TO BRING THE LEGION TUMBLING DOWN.

ONE WILL COME WITH FIRE IN HIS EYES,

TO PIERCE THROUGH THE VEIL OF WICKED LIES.

ONE WILL COME WITH FIRE IN HIS HEART,

TO OVERCOME ALL ODDS AND PLAY HIS PART.

ONE WILL COME WITH FIRE IN HIS HAND,

TO PURGE THE EVIL FROM THIS LAND.

ONE WILL COME TO PAY THE COST;

IF HE FAILS ALL IS LOST.

ONE WILL COME IN SUFFERING AND PAIN,

TO KNOW BETRAYAL AND BE WOUNDED AGAIN.

ONE WILL COME TO CHOOSE THE WAY;

ETERNAL DARKNESS OR THE ENDLESS DAY.

To Mum and Dad,
For always believing, always encouraging, always loving…
This book is for you.

First published in the UK in 2013 by Usborne Publishing Ltd., Usborne House, 83-85 Saffron Hill, London EC1N 8RT, England. www.usborne.com

Text copyright © Andrew Beasley, 2013

The right of Andrew Beasley to be identified as the author of this work has been asserted by him in accordance with the Copyright, Designs and Patents Act, 1988.

The name Usborne and the devices ♀ 🍥 are Trade Marks of Usborne Publishing Ltd.

Cover and inside illustrations by David Wyatt. Map by Ian McNee.

This is a work of fiction. The characters, incidents, and dialogues are products of the author's imagination and are not to be construed as real. Any resemblance to actual events or persons, living or dead, is entirely coincidental.

A CIP catalogue record for this book is available from the British Library.

ISBN 9781409544005   J MAMJJASOND/13   00828/04

Printed in Reading, Berkshire, UK.

THE BATTLES OF BEN KINGDOM

THE CLAWS OF EVIL

ANDREW BEASLEY

USBORNE

Contents

Day One: 20th December, 1891

Day Two: 21st December, 1891

Day Three: 22nd December, 1891

Day Four: 23rd December, 1891

 # Day Five: 24th December, 1891

Day Six: 25th December, 1891

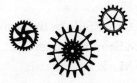

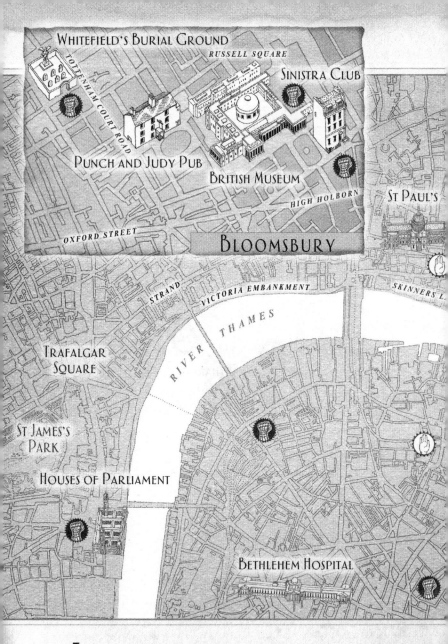

LONDON 1891

THE COOPER'S

BEN'S HOUSE

RATCLIFF HIGHWAY

LIVERPOOL ST STATION

Bank of England

ST PETER'S

OLD GRAVEL LANE

ALDGATE HIGH ST

NNON ST

JOLLY TAR PUB

OLD GRAVEL LANE

TOWER OF LONDON

St Katharine Docks

LONDON DOCKS

PICKLE HERRING ST

TOWER BRIDGE

OLD GRAVEL LANE

N

W — E

S

WATCHER CAMPS   LEGION ENTRANCES

DAY ONE
QUEEN VICTORIA'S LONDON –
20TH DECEMBER, 1891

# PROLOGUE

"London will soon be ours, ladies and gentlemen."

Mr. Sweet spoke and his audience listened. His voice was as deep and dark as tar, rising up from the barrel of his chest.

"We shall pluck out the beating heart of the British Empire and make it our plaything; a toy, to do with as we wish."

There were seven of them in all, including Mr. Sweet himself. They sat in a circle and talked treason, deciding how they might carve up the capital city between them. They called themselves the Council of Seven. A very modest title, Sweet thought, considering that the councils before them had shaped the world to please their own ends.

"And what shall we do with it, when it is ours?" pondered a hugely obese man, his jowls wobbling with anticipation, a thin trail of drool escaping from the corner of his mouth. "Eat it all?"

"What a foolish waste," said a woman dressed entirely in black, only her pale chin and bloodless lips visible beneath the shadows of her raven-feather hood. "Far better to suck it dry."

"No," said a second man, with parchment-dry skin stretched taut across his narrow skull, his long limbs hanging loosely over the edges of his chair. "We should enslave it, make it work for us."

"Burn it," purred a seductive woman in green, her fat pink tongue reaching out to caress her teeth. "It would be such a pretty sight." She clapped her hands in girlish glee. "We've put cities to the flame before. I should so like to see it for myself."

Mr. Sweet permitted the others to have their say, but soon shut out their prattling and focused instead on his own dream of the future; a dream which didn't include his six fellow conspirators. His vision was of London, ruled by a Council of one. Nanny had always said that he wasn't good at sharing.

Mr. Sweet was from a good family, in other words a wealthy one, and he had land and houses and more money than he could ever spend. He had power too; he was a Member of Parliament and a cabinet minister. But as any man with power would tell you, once you got a taste for it, there was never enough to go round.

It was Sweet who had called this meeting, and Sweet who had chosen the location. An elegant and yet foreboding building in Bloomsbury, The Sinistra Club was he most exclusive in all London and its members the most eccentric. If a man had been barred from every other establishment for his outrageous behaviour, or ungentlemanly conduct, then he might still be able to hang his hat at the Sinistra, providing he had deep enough pockets.

The club had one other unique feature which made it such a convenient place for the Council of Seven to meet. When you were discussing the overthrow of the government and the Queen herself, a certain level of discretion was required – even the Seven themselves knew that to repeat what was said would mean pain. Lots of pain. Probably death. But at the Sinistra Club, the staff could all be relied upon to keep absolutely mum. Because every servingmaid, footman, waiter and bottle-washer had two qualities that Sweet found desirable in a servant: they were both illiterate and mute. They could not record a single word that they overheard, and their tongues could not wag even if they wanted them to.

In every other respect, however, the Sinistra was the same as any of the basement clubs scattered across the city of London: oak-panelled, velvet lined, and reeking of money and cigars.

Sweet enjoyed the comfort of his chair and the elegance of his surroundings. The fire was burning brightly in the grate and keeping the bitter winter at bay; although these flames were obviously far too tame for the woman in green, he noted wryly.

She had been right: as the secret rulers of a society called the Legion, the Council of Seven had indeed turned cities to ash when it suited them. When the great city of Rome was consumed by fire in AD 64, it was the Legion, not Emperor Nero, who provided the spark. Mr. Sweet smiled, his teeth glistening in the gaslight. The footprints of the Legion stretched back for two thousand years if you knew where to look for them.

Blood was always a good clue.

Some members of the Legion had become quite famous in their own way, even if the army which they served remained a secret they took with them to their grave. Men whose names became a byword for brutality: Attila the Hun, who swept across Europe with unparalleled ferocity;

Vlad the Impaler; Ivan the Terrible; Maximilien Robespierre. The history books held them responsible for the deaths of hundreds of thousands, but Mr. Sweet knew that it was the Legion, led by the Council of Seven, to whom the credit truly belonged.

When the other voices in the room grew too grating for him to bear any longer, Mr. Sweet cleared his throat and rose to his feet. He was dressed like a gentleman, but his clothes strained to contain the heavyset body that lay beneath.

Very slowly, Sweet allowed his eyes to move around the circle, probing for signs of weakness, for the points of vulnerability where he would one day strike. It pleased him to see the Council of Seven flinch as his gaze touched them. They were the wickedest men and women in the land, and they were all afraid of him. Before he spoke, he paused to stroke his luxurious moustache. The movement did nothing to conceal his smile.

"Yes," continued Sweet, "London is ripe for the taking. The greatest weapon of the Legion is almost complete. I have discovered today that the final missing component, the last of the Coins, has come to light at last." There was a collective gasp at this revelation. "It will be ours," Sweet continued, "and then the whole of London will know the power of the Seven."

"But what about the Watchers?" said the youngest of their group, a vain, pampered man, with long, feminine fingers and foppish blond hair.

Mr. Sweet swung around and fixed him with the full force of his stare. The man shrank back, almost as if the blow were physical.

"The Watchers are a spent force." Sweet spat their name. "The pathetic followers of a failed cause, waiting for a saviour who will never come."

Yet even as he said those words, Mr. Sweet felt the tiny crack in his own armour, a chink that slowly filled with fear. *There will be no last-minute rescue for the enemies of the Legion*, he reassured himself. The Watchers had been abandoned, the Hand of Heaven was not coming to save them, Mr. Sweet was convinced of it.

And yet he couldn't stop the thin trickle of dread that was worming its way towards his soul.

CHAPTER 1

THE WEEPING MAN

"Ben Kingdom!"

The policeman's voice boomed out and every head in Old Gravel Lane turned.

Constable Wilde sounded cross and Ben couldn't blame him. A mouthful of fresh horse manure was enough to do that to anyone.

"Stop right where you are, you 'orrible boy!" Wilde shouted again. Ben hesitated, but one look at the constable's bespattered and beetroot-red face was enough to convince him that stopping was the last thing he wanted to do. Instead he pulled his billycock hat down nice and tight, took to his heels, and ran.

London's docks were the busiest in the world and the streets that surrounded them were awash with humanity. Some might call the people that lived and worked there "the dregs", but Ben was not the judgemental sort, and anyway, he was one of them. As nimble and lean as a whippet, Ben ducked and weaved his way through the crowd. Dodging elbows, squeezing between bodies, even getting down on his knees and crawling through the forest of legs, Ben knew that Wilde wouldn't catch him this time.

Poor bloke, thought Ben with a grin as he remembered his missile catching the bobby full in the face. *He's gonna be picking that out of his moustache till Christmas.*

All day, grey snow had been tumbling down out of the sky like ash and Ben's feet skidded on the cobbles as he made good his escape. His trousers were soaked through too, and his hands were wet and raw, but he soon left poor old Constable Wilde far behind and so it was a small enough price to pay.

Nine times out of ten, Ben was the very model of honesty. But during those rare lapses, it always seemed to be Constable Gabriel Wilde who arrived on the scene. It was Constable Wilde who had thrashed him after he broke the window of Langdale's tobacconists, and it was Wilde who caught him and thrashed him *again* after the unfortunate incident involving the butcher's dog, the sausages and the club-footed grocer.

In Ben's defence, he hadn't actually meant to hit Constable Wilde in the face; he was trying to knock off his helmet. And when he first came up with the idea, it was only going to be a snowball that he threw...but then the carthorse had been good enough to lay a stinking, steaming road-apple right there on the ground in front of him, and one thing led to another. It was pretty much the story of his life.

Satisfied that Wilde had definitely called it quits, Ben paused to set his hat at the right angle. A billycock was like a bowler hat, only a touch more dandy, and in Ben's opinion it had to be set just so. Happy, Ben grinned at his reflection in a shop window, shoved his throbbing hands back into his pockets and set off back towards Old Gravel Lane and home.

Night was beginning to fall now and the darkness brought a wicked edge to the wind that cut through his coat to the marrow in his bones. As he trudged through the quiet backstreets, a church bell chimed.

It was then that Ben saw the man.

The Weeping Man.

At least that was what the street kids called him.

Ben stopped dead and watched the figure from a

distance, trying to make out if it really could be him. Ghoulish curiosity getting the better of him, he took a step nearer.

At first, no one had even noticed that children were disappearing. If there was one thing that the East End wasn't short of, it was unwanted children. Kids went missing all the time. But then came the sightings and the stories and the whispers, until the length of Old Gravel Lane was abuzz with the news. *Beware the Man. The Man in Black who stalked the streets. The Weeping Man who came to take you away in the night.*

The descriptions of the villain were always the same: tall, dark. Deadly.

That ain't the half of it, thought Ben.

The figure that Ben had his eyes on was dressed all in black, as befitting a monster. He wore a long square-tailed coat which reached almost to the ground, and the broad shoulders beneath it made it abundantly clear that no street kid would have the strength to get away once he took hold of them. On his head sat the sort of hat which Ben always associated with undertakers. It was not a comforting image.

The other thing that all the accounts agreed upon was the noise that he made. "Unearthly", said a frightened clergyman who had heard it on his return from evensong.

"Disturbing", said a mother of three, who had not let her children out of the house since. Unnatural. Bone-chilling. A death rattle.

There were plenty of rumours about what he did with the children he took. But all anyone knew for certain was that kids were disappearing and nothing nice was happening to them.

Just so long as I'm not next, Ben told himself and he edged himself backwards into the hollow of a doorway, trying to become one with the gloom. When the cold wood was pressed hard against his back, he stopped. Then he waited. Not breathing...not moving...while all around him the snow continued its slow and remorseless assault. It was the harshest winter that anyone could remember and so there were plenty of ways for a scruffy street urchin like him to meet his Maker. Given the choice though, Ben had no wish to end his days as the latest victim of the Man in Black.

Ben studied him from the shadows. He was morbidly fascinated, and a little terrified too; although he would never own up to that. Jack the Ripper still cast his long shadow across the East End and Ben had no illusions about there being a happy ending to the story of the Weeping Man. But here he was. And a glimmer of opportunity was beginning to present itself to Ben, like a shiny sixpence begging for him to pick it up.

If, out of all of London, *he* was the one to identify the child snatcher, then he was bound to become famous. And *if* he was the one who could lead the bobbies to the beast's lair, then there surely had to be a reward in it for him. It was a brilliant plan, as far as he could see – the one tiny flaw being that it might cost him his own life trying. *Still, so far, so good, eh?*

Ben knew that he was being reckless. He knew that no one would come running if he screamed for help. *But in for a penny, in for a pound...*

Ben stuck his head out of the doorway for a better look. The Weeping Man was about twenty feet away now, taking a left into a dingy side street. Whatever he was doing, he obviously didn't want any witnesses.

What's your game? Ben wondered.

He picked up his feet and ran to the corner as silently as he could. He reached the entrance to the alley in time to see the Weeping Man stop dead in his tracks, sniffing the air. Ben froze too. He had allowed himself to be caught in the open, vulnerable and exposed. *If he turns around now...*

Inch by inch, Ben crept backwards, desperate for the protection that the wall could offer him. The snow crunching beneath his boots sounded as loud as cannon fire in his ears, and he winced with every step. He made it back behind the corner, but not before a shudder took hold of him so vigorously that it threatened to loosen the teeth in his head. And he knew that his trembling had nothing to do with the cold.

The Weeping Man stood motionless in the middle of the alley, unaware of Ben or unmoved by him. Ben studied him from his hiding place, transfixed; a rabbit stalking the fox.

Then, as suddenly as he had stopped, the Weeping Man lifted his head with a peculiar twitching jerk. It was an unnatural movement for a human, Ben thought; the angles were all wrong. He looked more like a dog cocking its neck and responding to a call which only he could hear; instructions from his master.

But whose voice was he listening to?

Ben went rigid and held his breath tightly in his chest, next to his hammering heart. Had he been heard? He grimaced as he imagined what was coming to him if the Weeping Man turned round.

Then the sound of the man's tears echoed down the alleyway and there was no doubt left in Ben's mind: he was in the presence of a killer.

He felt the sound as much as heard it; the physical manifestation of a soul in torment. The sobbing came from somewhere very deep within the man, or so it seemed to Ben. Beginning with a low growl, it built with each shuddering gasp until it was finally released as a volcano of grief. Ben could almost feel the pressure mounting inside the Weeping Man until there was nowhere for it to go except to explode to the surface.

There was so much sadness in those sobs. Such pain. Such remorse.

But there was anger too, and that was what scared Ben the most.

The howling rage.

Get out of here, and get out now. That was what the sensible part of Ben's mind was telling him to do. And not for the first time, Ben wished that once in a while he would listen to the advice that it gave, instead of always following the other voice, the one that insisted on the exact opposite. *Don't be chicken-hearted*, it said. *Get a closer look. Looking never hurt anyone.*

Mind made up, Ben Kingdom inched forwards in the hope of getting a really good look-see.

Easy does it, Benny boy.

He had halved the distance between them when his foot caught against an empty bottle and sent it rattling across the cobbles.

It wasn't exciting any more.

It was dark. It was late.

And he was alone in a very bad place.

Fear filled Ben's throat as he realized what he had done. He glanced around at the tight corridor of the alleyway, filthy tenements on either side. In his curiosity, he had allowed himself to be led away down Skinners Lane. *Stupid, stupid, stupid,* he cursed himself. Everybody knew that you didn't go down Skinners Lane at night unless you had a death wish. *You really are on your own now, son.*

To Ben's horror, at that moment the Weeping Man cocked his head and very slowly turned around. He took a step in Ben's direction.

Then another.

Ben couldn't move now, even if he wanted to.

Twelve paces away.

Eleven.

Why can't I run? Ben screamed inside. *Why can't I just run?*

Ten paces.

Nine.

Then, as Ben watched, a heap of unwanted rags – bundled up, left to rot at the side of the street – began to stir with life. The Weeping Man kneeled over the tattered remnants, stretched out his hand and, from beneath the surface, from under the filth and the grey stain of snow, another hand emerged, tiny and pale. Slowly, frail fingers reached out and clasped the Weeping Man's. An arm like a stick followed that hand, and then the form of a girl, fragile and lost.

It was Molly Marbank. Sweet little Molly Marbank, whose father worked with Ben's father at the docks. Or at least he had until he missed seeing the beam that was swinging towards him, sweeping Mr. Marbank's legs one way and his soul straight on to glory. After that Molly was orphaned and alone, and everyone assumed that she had gone to the workhouse.

Only Ben now knew that Molly was here, hand in hand with the Weeping Man.

The girl by his side, the Weeping Man rose to his feet and turned to leave.

And in that instant, Ben knew that he had been seen.

For the first time, Ben saw fully the face of death. The Weeping Man was much younger than he had expected: clean-shaven, square-jawed, with an almost aristocratic face, framed by tumbling dark hair. Ben saw soft cheeks, slick with tears. He saw a broad mouth, smiling. He saw a sword beneath the folds of the black coat, long and wickedly sharp. He saw eyes as deep and dark as wells. Ancient eyes, that had seen secret and terrible things.

And those eyes saw him.

The Weeping Man addressed him from the darkness. "I shall be coming for you, Benjamin Kingdom," he said.

And then, at last, Ben could run.

CHAPTER 2

MUDLARKS, CHANCERS AND THIEVES

Ben ran until his chest ached and each breath burned like a mouthful of hot coals. As his legs began to give way, he forced himself to put one more turn in the road between himself and the Weeping Man, before finally collapsing against a wall, exhausted and shaking.

That was a close one, he told himself.

His hands were tingling, he realized, a strange pins-and-needles feeling that was more than just the cold. He flexed his fingers, trying to make them feel normal again, but the odd prickling ache continued. It was something that he had experienced all his life: a throbbing, burning sensation that he couldn't explain. All he knew was there were times, normally when he was angry or scared or stirred by deep emotions, when he thought that his hands might burst into flame.

He rolled his hands into tight fists as he thought about poor Molly, and they burned even brighter. He hadn't raised a finger to save her.

Some friend he'd turned out to be.

He should have attacked the Weeping Man and rescued her. Maybe he could have distracted him somehow and given her a chance to escape? Or at the very least he could have shouted out; bought her another second of freedom.

Then he remembered the sword.

The sorry truth was that the only way it could have played out differently was for there to be two dead children instead of one. But truth or not, that didn't stop Ben from blaming himself.

He still couldn't get over the way that Molly had just upped and gone with the Weeping Man. Ben had been petrified and yet Molly had shown no sign of fear. On the contrary, the expression on her face had been one of absolute peace as she'd taken his outstretched hand. It made no sense to Ben. Most likely she had merely been numbed with cold and past caring.

All that Ben had been able to do for her in that final

moment was to plead with her through his eyes: *Don't go*, he had urged her. *Don't go, Molly.*

It didn't feel like enough to him. But he didn't cry.

Ben had seen a lot of death already in his young life, but there was only one person that he mourned for. A sharp pain pierced his heart as he thought of her. A single tear appeared and for a second it lay on his cheek like a jewel before he scrubbed it crossly away.

That's enough of that, he told himself sharply. He brushed himself down, set his billycock hat back on his head at what he considered to be a jaunty angle, and put some of the usual swagger back into his step. He might just have been scared out of his wits, but he still had his reputation to think of. He *was* Ben Kingdom, after all.

Soon Ben was back on the relative safety of his home turf and feeling more like himself, the burning in his hands gone for now. He paused in front of Ricolleti's, the Italian grocery and provision store, and for a moment he studied his reflection, framed by cases of tinned meat and barrels of dark tea.

Ben was pretty much like all the other boys he knew; older than his years. His eyes were big and blue, though they often looked tired, and his teeth were all fairly white, which was something to boast about. But the thing that made him stand out from the crowd was his hair: a mane of red-gold that some said made him look like a lion. Others said that redheads were full of anger and bad news. Ben denied this fervently. Mind you, anyone who found it funny to call him "carrots" would get a thick lip for their efforts as quick as they could blink.

Aching with cold, Ben turned up the collar of his coat and shoved his hands deep into his pockets. Though he would never admit it, he couldn't shake the memories of Skinners Lane. He needed something to distract himself and so he pointed his feet in the direction of the Jolly Tar public house. There was a man there that he needed to see.

It was never quiet near the London Docks and as he got closer to the inn, he took comfort in the presence of the burly coal whippers, ballast-heavers, sailmakers and watermen, all brushing shoulders. And then the boys like himself, causing mischief and getting in the way; mudlarks, chancers and thieves. *And me the biggest chancer of them all,* thought Ben.

He picked up his step as the Jolly Tar came in sight. This was where he always came when he needed to escape from the harsh realities of his life.

Because this was where he would find old Jago Moon.

CHAPTER 3

CLAW CARTER

Bones.

In trays. In cases. Beneath glass. Each one scrutinized, identified, listed, labelled and annotated. The elongated claws of burrowing mammals, the massive thigh of a great cat, the horn of a narwhal, the jaws of a Nile crocodile. The ivory of the ages, all the flesh stripped away. One entire wall was devoted to craniums and brain cases: a wall of skulls. No eyes in their sockets, no tongues in their mouths, but teeth aplenty, and even the most dim-witted idiot to come stumbling in through the door, broom in hand, could imagine that the beasts were living still. Living and breathing and snarling. And feeding.

There were no windows in this room and the only light came from a flickering oil lamp on the desk, feeding the shadows that lurked in the corners and grew fat. If the man seated there alone was in the least bit troubled by his surroundings, he didn't show it. In fact the opposite appeared to be true; here was a man who seemed entirely at home in this catacomb, surrounded only by the remnants of the dead.

What are we anyway, thought Professor James Carter, *if not fragile flesh hung upon a tree of bones?*

Professor Carter examined the tray of bones before him. They purported to be the fingers of martyrs and saints. He snorted at the idea; he had never found any man worthy of the title. He chose one at random and brought it close to his eye. *Did you perform miracles while you lived?* he wondered. Dismissively, he tossed it back with the others. *I think not.*

Carter examined his own hands. The left was broad palmed and strong fingered, the flesh bronzed by foreign winds. The right? Well, that was different. His arm ended in a stump just below where his wrist used to be, and beyond that was bone of an entirely different sort.

If he had been a pirate, Carter might have chosen to replace his missing hand with a hook. But he was not a pirate. He was a professor of history at the British

Museum, and so he chose a different sort of prosthesis altogether.

He held it up and admired it in the lamplight: a wicked sickle of bone; a claw to be precise. A miracle designed for ripping and cutting and slashing. Before time began it had belonged to a mighty hunter, a dinosaur, the great *Megalosaurus*. Now it belonged to him. It made him the man he was.

There was a hesitant knock on the door and he swivelled in his chair to face it. "Come," he said, and a ragged boy tumbled in, breathing heavily.

"There's been a finding, sir," said the boy, still panting. "Something that we think you need to come and look at."

Carter nodded in response; perhaps he wouldn't have to wait much longer for the power he desired. He paused to pull on a long leather trench coat, as brown and weather-beaten as the man himself. "A finding, you say?" He turned to the boy, and grinned like a skull. "Then that must be a job for Claw Carter."

CHAPTER 4

THE TOUCH

At the Jolly Tar, Ben was met with raucous laughter and a grey fog of tobacco spilling out of the door. Inside he found the usual mass of unwashed bodies and, after a second of searching, caught sight of Mr. Moon, sitting hunched over a table in his usual corner beside the fire. Ben eased his way through the drinkers and lingerers, taking great care not to jog any elbows on his way; it was more than his life was worth to spill someone's drink.

Far from his home in East India, a morose and muscular lascar stood at the bar, drinking steadily. Beside him stood a coal porter with biceps the size of hocks of ham.

A monkey chattered angrily from its vantage point on the lascar's shoulder, alternately picking at its fleas and spitting in the coal porter's glass. If the porter's glazed eyes ever cleared up long enough for him to notice, then a right old heave-to was definitely on the cards.

Ben hurried past.

As silently as he could, Ben eased himself into the seat opposite Moon, taking care so that his chair did not make a sound against the flagstone floor.

"Good evening, Master Kingdom," said Jago Moon.

"Good evening, Mr. Moon," Ben replied, amazed at how the old man saw him coming every time.

With two blind eyes, Jago Moon regarded him across the table. "I've been expecting you," he said in a voice of gravel.

Ben was taken aback, but not wrong-footed; he was a regular customer, after all. He eyed Moon's satchel and wondered what treasures it contained this time.

In defiance of his blindness, Jago Moon was a seller of second-hand books, specializing in lurid tales just suited to an imagination like Ben's. Moon always had a supply of the cheap cloth-bound pamphlets that stuck-up toffs called the "penny dreadfuls". Ben read them greedily and knew their names by heart: *Black Knight of the Road*, *The Skeleton Burglar*, *Starlight Sal*, *The Resurrection Men*...

Stories about villains and robbers and bodysnatchers and terrible doings in the night; what could be so dreadful about that?

It would horrify old "Cowpat" Cowper, the Sunday school teacher who had taught Ben his letters, to know that he was wasting the precious gift of reading on such tawdry tales. But then Cowpat Cowper probably went home to a nice warm house and a nice safe life and didn't need to escape from his reality quite so much as Ben.

"What have you got for me today, Mr. Moon?" said Ben, getting ready to slide his well-worn coin across the table. "Pirates? Highwaymen?"

From over by the bar, an angry voice rose above the throng. "Is that your monkey gobbin' in my rum?"

Ben knew that was his signal to leave; all he wanted was to get his book and get out before things turned nasty. But Moon seemed to be taking for ever, rummaging in his satchel. Eventually he drew out a dog-eared old volume entitled *The Boy Burglar*.

"That'll do nicely," said Ben, reaching for the book with one hand and pushing a farthing forwards with the other. "A pleasure doing business with you, sir." But even as Ben made to get up, shoving his chair away with the back of his legs, Jago Moon's fingers accidentally brushed against Ben's. In that instant, Ben felt an invisible power pass from him to Moon and they both flung their hands up in shock, struck by strange lightning.

"I'm sorry, Mr. Moon," Ben began, "I don't—"

Ben's words were cut short as Moon's hand whipped out and clasped Ben's forearm tight. Ben winced and made to pull away, but Moon was surprisingly strong and dragged him down until their faces were level. The milky orbs of Moon's blind eyes rolled in his skull as he breathed doom upon Ben. In spite of the stifling heat, Ben's blood turned to ice in his veins.

"Listen here and listen good," Moon hissed urgently, his lips so close that Ben could feel the rasp of stubble against his face. "You've got the Touch, lad." Moon made it sound as if this was a good thing. "Your life ain't never gonna be the same again. You've been chosen, Ben. The Weeping Man is coming for you."

CHAPTER 5

A PIECE
OF HISTORY

Professor Carter swept through the streets. The tails of his coat billowed out behind him like wings. The air was bitter, although not as cold as it had been in the mountains of Nepal. When a man had travelled, it gave him a certain perspective on things, Carter mused. It allowed him to see the bigger picture.

The boy ran on ahead of him, eager to please. He went by the name of Jimmy Dips, a pickpocket by trade. Carter was a collector, and in order for there to be a collection, many things needed to be found. He had decided a long time ago that it was better not to ask where or how, but to quietly employ the services of boys like Jimmy, who could sniff out items in dark places. Some objects, of course, were worth more than others. It was that possibility that made him leave the comfort of the museum on such a night as this.

After all, how often did a man get the chance to hold an object that had once altered the course of history and was about to change the world again?

Jimmy Dips scampered to the corner of the street, looked both ways and then rushed back to the professor's side. He reminded Carter of a ferret; his face was all nose, constantly twitching and tasting the air.

"Nearly there now, Professor," said Jimmy.

"I know," Claw Carter snapped. There was a limit to how much mindless enthusiasm he could stomach.

The Punch and Judy public house was only a short walk from the British Museum and it was a venue that he had often found suitable for conversations of a private nature. There were no lights showing when they arrived, so Carter marched over to the door and knocked on it smartly with his claw.

There was the sound of bolts being drawn back from inside, followed by a hushed voice: "Is that you?"

"Who else do you think it might be?" said Carter, flinging the door open and seeing no reason to keep his voice down. "Father Christmas?"

The fat innkeeper looked suitably chastened. Jimmy Dips could not conceal his smile.

"She's down there," said the innkeeper, pointing the way to the cellar.

With Jimmy trailing in his wake, Carter descended the steps and found a girl sitting in a corner behind a round oak table. Her delicate arms were spread out across the back of her chair, a picture of feline ease.

"Good evening, Miss Johnson," said Carter.

"Good evening, Professor," she purred.

Of all the gutter rats and street thieves that Professor Carter knew, Ruby Johnson was the most audacious and the least expendable. She had chestnut-brown hair, chopped in a jagged, almost boyish style, and eyes the shape of almonds.

"Drink?" she asked.

"I'm not in the mood."

"I meant for me," said Ruby.

Carter threw back his head and laughed. "A drink for the lady, if you would be so kind, Jimmy." He snapped the fingers of his good hand. "In a clean glass."

Jimmy hurried off.

"Now," said the professor, all business, "you have something for me?"

Ruby reached into the pocket of her velvet jacket and

brought out a small object, wrapped in a jeweller's cloth. The professor was impatient to see and took it from her swiftly. He held it for a moment, clutching it tightly in his fist, before relaxing and placing it on the table in front of him, then gently peeling back the corners of the cloth to expose the treasure within.

Even in the gloom, Ruby could see the glint in his eyes.

"The lamp, quickly, bring it over," he urged.

He began to examine the object, hardly daring to believe what he might have found. He didn't even touch it at first, he simply allowed it to sit safely on its cloth while he extracted the truth from it.

It was the right size. Small and round, no bigger than one inch in diameter.

"How did you know that this was one of them?" he asked, his eyes not leaving the table.

"I didn't," she shrugged. "But it matched the description you gave us and so…"

That description had proved utterly useless so far. He could hardly believe some of the rubbish that they had brought him, thinking it was the find of the century. But this? It was the right metal. Silver, approximately eighty per cent pure, he would say. It certainly appeared to be a Tyrian Shekel; the approved coin of the Jewish temple tax. He examined it further.

Ruby looked on; the cat that'd got the cream.

Carter's mouth was suddenly dry. The inscription was accurate. The decoration was of the right period too; an eagle with its claw on a ship's rudder. The edges were imperfect, but that was only to be expected; it had been crimped from a silver sheet, not poured into a mould. That was how they made coins in the Roman Empire nearly two thousand years ago.

Jimmy returned with Ruby's drink, but neither she nor Carter paid him any notice. Carefully, Professor Carter picked up the silver coin by the edges and held it closer to the light.

"Do you know what this is?" Carter asked.

"A Roman coin, like you asked for."

"Oh no." He shook his head slowly. "It is so much more than that. This is a piece of history. There were thirty of these coins in the beginning, and we, the Legion, already hold twenty-nine of them. Some people call them the Coins of Blood." He smiled. "I call them an opportunity."

Of course, like any army, the Legion had its ranks. Carter was not cannon fodder like Jimmy Dipps and all the other ragamuffins. Carter was a knight commander, but he too was a man under authority. His orders were to pass the Coin onwards and upwards to Mr. Sweet; respectable Member of Parliament by day, schemer and murderer by night. And orders were orders, he supposed; except the expression "finders keepers" kept springing to mind. If *he* was the one with the power of the Coins, then Mr. Sweet would be answering to *him*.

The power to control men, to bend them to your will. *Who doesn't dream of that?* he wondered.

He pinched the coin lightly between forefinger and thumb, noticing the slightest tremble in his hand. Then he turned the coin over and his triumph turned to ashes in his mouth.

Instead of the image of the Phoenician god Melkart, he saw the fat face of the Emperor Tiberius winking back at him. He'd got the wrong man.

"*No!*" The word escaped his lips in a roar of disappointment. Carter hurled the worthless coin away with savage disgust before scanning the room for another means to vent his rage. Jimmy Dips cowered when Carter's eyes fell upon him. Even the unflappable Ruby Johnson averted her gaze, her face grey.

"It's not the one," Carter snarled as he leaped to his feet, and he brought his claw down across the table in a single vicious blow, cleaving it in two.

CHAPTER 6

THE PROPHECY

The Jolly Tar wasn't all that jolly any more. The air had turned blue with curses. Glass broke. Fists flew. The monkey screamed.

Ben had more on his mind than a bit of monkey spit though. His head was spinning and he needed to get out. He weaved his way through the crowd as swiftly as he could, doing his best to avoid getting punched in the process.

When he made it to the door and the frosty night air hit him, he drank it down in great gulps. What was happening to his life? First he had seen little Molly fall prey to the Weeping Man. Then he'd managed to single himself out as the next victim in the process. And he couldn't even begin to understand what had happened when his fingers touched Jago Moon's, but he did know that he wanted to get as far away from the crazy old man as possible.

He remembered Moon's mad eyes and ominous words and began to feel his head reeling again.

Pull yourself together, he told himself firmly, and after a final determined drag of cold air, he drew himself up straight and rolled his shoulders back.

To his disappointment, he realized that he hadn't even managed to pick up his book in all the confusion, but there was no way that he was going back in to face Moon again. At least he'd managed to pocket his farthing though, and with that thought he began to head for home. True, it wouldn't be much warmer there than it was out here in the street, and it stank worse than a tramp's armpit in August, but home was still home.

As he walked back through the snow he let his mind wander through his best-loved stories. Mummies... vampires...Spring-heeled Jack...the Red-Legged Scissor Man... Anything to take his mind off the real horror that was encroaching on his life from every direction, he thought grimly.

His imagination was always full of the mysterious and other-worldly; something he must have got from his mum, he supposed. After all, she had believed in a good, caring God and guardian angels who watched out for you…and what could be more incredible than that?

Was there some divine protector looking down on him? he wondered. *Fat chance*, he thought and laughed out loud at such a ridiculous idea.

Silently, the Watcher on the rooftop followed Ben's movements, just as the Weeping Man had ordered her to do.

Lucy Lambert had seen the boy as soon as he left the Jolly Tar. He was just like all the others she had observed: oblivious. Oblivious to the truth about the world he was living in. Oblivious to the war which was raging all around him.

Totally oblivious to the role that he was destined to play.

The Weeping Man hadn't said as much, but it was obvious to Lucy that this was more than just a routine survey-and-report mission. The tone of his voice had implied that this boy was important somehow, and now that she saw Ben Kingdom in the flesh, the ferociously ginger hair was something of a giveaway.

Lucy knew the words of the prophecy as well as any other Watcher, and they came unbidden to her mind.

One will come to lead the fight, to defeat the darkness,
bring the triumph of the light.
One will come with fire as his crown,
to bring the Legion tumbling down.
One will come with fire in his eyes,
to pierce through the veil of wicked lies.
One will come with fire in his heart,
to overcome all odds and play his part.
One will come with fire in his hand,
to purge the evil from this land...

She stopped then. The final verses always terrified her.

If this Ben Kingdom really was the one, then the final verses would terrify him too.

With one hand resting against the chimney, Lucy leaned forward to look at Ben more closely. There had been false alarms before; other boys that the Watchers had put their hopes in, only to have those hopes turn to dust. Lucy flicked back her head to set free the hair that was blocking her vision. If the prophecy had spoken of a *girl* instead, then the battle would have been over and done with by now. She decided to raise the point the next time she had an audience with Mother Shepherd, the leader of the Watchers; she was a woman, she would understand.

Although the snow had eased off, the wind was as sharp as a butcher's knife and it sliced around her legs, willing her to fall. She shifted her stance slightly, using her skyboots to get a better hold on the slick roof tiles, feeling the ice crunch reassuringly beneath their studded rubber soles. She didn't feel any danger of slipping; she was a Watcher and the Watchers were trained to go where others would never dare.

She didn't feel cold either. Well, perhaps that wasn't quite true; she *was* cold, but she wasn't freezing. She wore the Watchers' uniform: a long trench coat; leather gauntlets; brass-rimmed goggles so that she could see in any weather; and a light bag slung across her shoulder containing her other, more specialized, equipment. She had tied a scarf around her mouth too. She looked quite dashing, she thought. The one thing that spoiled the look was the livid red scar which ran down her right cheek and the patch that covered the socket where her eye used to be.

Ben Kingdom was on the move and she ran a parallel course along the rooftop, keeping low, like a cat. It was merely a precaution; she had never been seen before. No one in London ever looked up.

Beneath her gaze, Benjamin laughed at some joke of his own. Oblivious *and* foolish, she decided.

Only a fool would walk into danger with a laugh on his lips.

As much as he tried to distract himself, Ben's thoughts could not stray far from the night's events. It had been a busy few hours, and no mistake. He wished he could believe that Mr. Moon had been rambling drunk. He wished that Molly had stayed hidden. He wished that he could forget the way that the Weeping Man had called his name. He wished that it wasn't Christmas time and he didn't feel the pain of his memories. But as his father never tired of telling him, wishing didn't make it so.

All the way home, Ben sensed that he was being followed; there was an itch inside his skull that told him he wasn't safe yet. Trying his best to make it look nonchalant, he stole a glimpse over his shoulder. The street was far from empty. He saw a couple of sailors, rolling home on sea legs lubricated with ale; a downstairs maid, clearly out after her curfew and regretting it; some street boys like himself, killing a few more hours with monkeyshines and skylarks; a matchstick seller, praying for one last sale before bedding down. What there wasn't, as far as Ben could see, was a man in a long black coat, carrying a sword and looking for him.

He chose to believe that he had imagined the feeling that he was being stalked, but by the time he reached his front door, his nerves felt as frayed as old rope. With one more furtive glance, he turned the key in the lock and he was in, almost tumbling over the doorstep to be swallowed up by the shadows of the hall.

Made it.

Ben enjoyed his triumph for a whole second before he realized he was not alone. A deep voice spoke to him from the darkness of the hallway, and the hairs stood proud on his neck.

"What's this, Ben Kingdom?"

A red glow on the stairs and the soft crackle of burning tobacco led Ben's eyes to a filthy old pipe, and behind that, sucking away at its stem, a filthy old man.

To his relief, Ben realized that it wasn't the Weeping Man waiting to take him away, or Jago Moon with more helpful messages of impending doom; it was only Mr. Wachowski, the ageing Polish sailor who shared their crowded boarding house.

"Made you jump, didn't I?" said Mr. Wachowski, who clearly thought this was a joke worthy of the finest music hall. By means of an encore he followed it up with a phlegm-rattling cough that was the best laugh he could manage with the lungs he had left.

"No," Ben lied defiantly. "You didn't."

Jago Moon followed Benjamin Kingdom all the way from the Jolly Tar, only content that he was safe when he heard the front door click shut.

Stupid boy, he thought to himself; so wrapped up in his stories and world of make-believe that he didn't realize he was already part of the greatest adventure of them all. *You even need a blind old man to make sure you get home in one piece.*

Although his eyes were worthless, showing him a murky world of shadows and ghosts, Jago Moon's hearing was exceptional. Since his sight had been stolen from him many years ago, he had trained his mind and body every day, learning to detect even the most subtle nuance in the air around him. He was able to pick out one voice in a crowded room and know how far away the talker was. He could picture what they were wearing by the sound of their clothes: silk swished, cotton chafed, linen rasped, crinoline rustled, wool muffled. He knew a spider was crawling up a wall by the drumming of its legs; could tell the difference between more than a dozen different tobaccos just by the sound of their burning.

Moon had also discovered that a man's footstep was as unique as his face. Length of stride told him everything he needed to know about height; the heaviness of the footfall revealed weight, build, balance and bearing. A nervous man had a hesitant step; a self-assured man walked with a confident stride, his heels striking the ground like the snap of a whip. Soldiers walked differently to sailors, to costermongers, to bankers, to idlers.

Ben had been easy to follow and, from the sound of his gait, some of his usual cockiness had left him, which had to be a good thing. He was wearing the same boots that he always did, the ones that were too big and slopped around the skinny feet inside. He had walked home cautiously, putting more weight on his toes than normal. Three times he had scuffed on the cobbles when he'd tried to hurry; another telltale sign of someone who was scared.

Ben was right to be afraid, thought Moon. If the Watchers knew his name then the Legion wouldn't be far behind.

Moon smiled with the few teeth he owned. He had jumped out of his skin when he felt the raw power flowing from Ben's hand. There had always been a sneaky suspicion in the back of Moon's mind that there was something special about the boy, but he had never thought that Ben Kingdom might be the one to fulfil the prophecy.

Me ears are good, but even I can't hear hair colour, he thought, his smile widening.

Benjamin Kingdom, who'd have thought it? How might a cocky lad with a smart tongue and a knack for finding trouble be transformed into the Hand of Heaven, the leader whose wisdom and self-sacrifice would guide the Watchers to glory? It was very much the Watcher way to choose the least likely to rise the highest, but this might be stretching the point: there wasn't a soul the entire length of Old Gravel Lane who had a good word to say about the lad.

Jago Moon laughed to himself; he didn't suppose people had much that was pleasant to say about a blind old madman like him, either.

A furtive dragging sound from the far end of the Lane snapped him from his reverie. In his experience, slow sounds spoke of stealth and secrets. He focused his keen ears; there it was again. The grating of metal on cobblestones; a manhole cover being lifted. Instinctively Moon grasped his cane more tightly. The Legion had arrived. Like insects, thought Moon, crawling out from beneath a stone.

Although he knew that Mother Shepherd was certain to disapprove, Moon couldn't stop himself from hating the Legion. The Watchers were governed by truth, the Legion was ruled by lies. The Watchers rescued people, comforted them, helped them to be set free from the chains of poverty, hopelessness or despair; the Legion used people, exploited their burdens, fuelled the fire of their bitterness until they were angry at the whole world.

And then there was the small matter of the Legion wanting to unleash the powers of Hell and usher in a reign of evil on earth.

The Watchers believed in love, but when it came to the Legion, Moon was an advocate of *tough* love. He gripped the handle of his cane and silently hoped that a Legionnaire would stray within swinging distance.

Moon's ears told him that there was a Watcher on guard on the roof above Ben's room. He could hear the flapping of their trench coat, the crunch of their skyboots on the icy slates. The footfalls were very light so it must be one of the younger ones, he reasoned. Probably a girl, judging by their grace. His grin grew wider. He didn't envy the Legionnaire who tried to mess with a Watcher girl; they were all as tough as hobnailed boots.

He stood in the shadows, braced for action; he was no pushover either. The aching cold and the arthritis gnawing at his knuckles had put him in the mood for cracking a few Legion skulls. It might be a good night after all.

CHAPTER 7

THE GHOST LIGHT

Ben watched with a mixture of fascination and disgust as Mr. Wachowski's laughter dislodged something wet inside the man's lungs. Sitting on the bottom step of the stairs, the old man rocked back and forth, hacking and coughing, until he finally shifted the blockage and, with a look of triumph, spat it out onto the tiled hall floor.

"Mr. Wachowski!" A woman's voice rang out from the direction of the kitchen and the old man went stiff at the sound. "Mr. Wachowski," their landlady, Mrs. McLennon, continued, "are you spitting in my house again?"

"No," said Mr. Wachowski in his rich Polish accent,

and then smiled at Ben at a lie shared, showing him a row and a half of brown teeth.

"Well, I will certainly not be the one mopping it up. This is a clean house –" she pronounced it "hoos" in her Scottish brogue – "a Godly house," she continued, "and I will not have blasphemers and heathens spitting on my tiles."

As she emerged from the kitchen to inspect the evidence for herself, Ben bid them both a quick "Goodnight". He left them arguing in the hallway, Mrs. McLennon quoting the scriptures and Mr. Wachowski mumbling the filthiest obscenities that a Polish sailor could think of.

Ben smiled as he climbed the creaking stairs. Home sweet home.

The ground floor of the house was all taken by the widow, McLennon, who lived alone with a mean-tempered cat who ate better than Ben did. In the basement there was Mr. Wachowski, who had arrived in London as a young man with a great vision of importing Polish pickles and becoming rich. Sadly for him, somewhere along the line the plan had fallen short and so his life now mainly consisted of smoking and spitting.

On the first landing there were two rooms and two families. The longest serving residents of the two were the

O'Rourkes: Mr. O'Rourke, a coal whipper at the docks, whose skin was ingrained with black even after his Sunday wash; Mrs. O'Rouke, a sturdy and well-built woman, who scrubbed doorsteps for richer women but never seemed to resent them for it; and four little O'Rourkes, Jimmy (seven), Jenny (six), Catherine (three) and Stephen (two). "Plus two in Heaven, one more on the way," Mrs. O'Rourke had told Ben last week, with a pat on her belly that was beginning to round. She had smiled at him as she always did, but there had been a tear in her eye, and Ben hadn't been sure whether it was a happy tear or a sad one.

The O'Rourkes brought two welcome sounds to the house: laughter and an Irish fiddle. But their neighbours in the next room brought only one sound: shouting. Mr. Viney shouted at Mrs. Viney because no one would take him on at the docks again. Mrs. Viney shouted at Mr. Viney because other men could find work if they wanted to. Mr. Viney shouted at the boys (Walter and William) because they were always underfoot. Mrs. Viney shouted at the boys because they were breaking their mother's heart with their wicked ways. Walter and William shouted at each other because it was the only thing their parents had taught them to do.

The first floor was the noisy floor.

Ben climbed the last set of stairs to the attic room and then paused outside the door. He could hear two sets of snores and entered as quietly as he could. He wasn't bothered about waking his brother, Nathaniel, but he didn't want to trouble his father. He crept in and took a position by the window. He needed to know that the Weeping Man wasn't out there, waiting for his moment to strike.

Outside, the storm had found new strength from somewhere and snow was hurling itself against the cracked window. What they called the curtain, which was actually the remains of an old nightshirt tacked above the glass, billowed in and out with every gust. He strained his eyes to find a figure in the storm and found none, but still did not feel safe.

Jack Frost had begun to trace his long fingers across the inside of the window. The water in the jug on the washstand was frozen solid and so was whatever his family had left in the chamber pot. On their thin mattresses, his father and brother were both unmoving. Ben turned away from the window and watched them, their clouds of breath the only sign that they were alive. *I'm keeping my hat on again tonight*, he thought and, pulling it down tight, he wrapped his coat around him and prepared to settle down.

He drew up his blanket, which, as always, was slightly damp and smelled vaguely of cabbage. His own sleeping mat was especially lumpy, mainly due to his secret stash of books. He knew what his father, Jonas, would say about him spending money on books when they didn't have enough to eat.

Ben lay down so that he was facing Jonas and studied him in the ghost light of the moon.

His pa had a good face, Ben thought; a strong face. The lines on it were signs of determination, endurance and courage. Jonas's arms were big from lifting, his shoulders big from carrying. And his heart was big from giving. There was so much that Benjamin wanted to talk about with his father. About books, yes, and life and the future; all his hopes and dreams.

And he stopped there.

There would be no talking, he knew. Jonas Kingdom had never forgiven his son for the cruellest crime committed against their family.

"Goodnight, Pa," Ben said quietly. "I love you."

No one heard his words and no one replied.

Benjamin Kingdom closed his eyes and did not sleep.

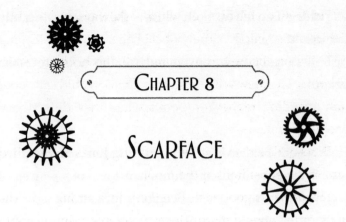

CHAPTER 8

SCARFACE

At some point, Ben must have drifted off.

The room could hardly have been colder; the curtain had frozen to the window pane, his blanket was as stiff as leather. All Ben wanted to do was to stay asleep a while longer, but something was tugging him back to wakefulness.

There was a noise.

Ben listened intently, straining his ears to pick up the sound. It came again, a scuffling from somewhere above his head. What was it? Rats in the rafters again? He shuddered at the thought. There was something about those fat bodies and naked pink tails that really disturbed him. Nasty beady eyes, teeth made for biting, claws for scratching. Ben felt his body tense at the thought. *Anything but rats.*

Bolt upright now, he waited for the noise to come again.

Far beneath Benjamin's feet, two rats were scurrying his way. They were in a secret tunnel, just one of a warren of secret tunnels that was the Legion's hidden home below the London streets. And behind those rats, moving softly and with purpose, came two young Legionnaires. They went by the names of Mickelwhite and Bedlam, and it would be hard to find a less likely couple. Mickelwhite was tall, lean, pale, aristocratic; Bedlam was short, squat, dark, as rough as a tosher's dog. The only thing they shared was hate.

They had their various reasons, they had their own stories. But they had made the same choice: join the Legion.

They were two boys who had promised to give their all for the Council of Seven, two soldiers in a war where the prize was more than they could possibly comprehend; two Legionnaires obeying orders, scouting out the enemy. Most nights they did the same. Hunt for Watchers. Look for signs of light.

Snuff them out.

Not so far above Benjamin's head, Lucy Lambert maintained her silent vigil. The wind tugged at her long coat, trying its best to catch her with her guard down and throw her off the roof to a death of cobblestones and shattered bones.

The Watcher did not flinch. She and her kind lived on the rooftops of London. The high places were their domain. Friends with gargoyles and pigeons, they spent their days amid the chimney pots, turrets and towers, only touching solid ground when their mission demanded it. What was a little wind and snow to her?

Lucy had often wondered what the Hand would be like when he was finally revealed. She found it hard to reconcile the image she had built in her mind with the swaggering boy that she was standing guard over. Ben Kingdom didn't appear to be special or powerful. He didn't even come across as especially bright.

Although he is sort of handsome, she supposed…but then she dismissed the idea, angry with herself for even having thought it.

Lucy clenched her quarterstaff more tightly, pumping some fresh blood into her fingers in case she needed to defend the stupid boy in a hurry. Time would tell if he was worth it.

One thing was for certain, a storm was coming. Day after day, the Legion were becoming more powerful, and soon they would make their move. There were even whispers that the last of the lost Coins had been found. Open war was on its way and the Watchers were prepared.

Lucy spun her staff from hand to hand, practising the lunge, slash and jab that would have any Legionnaire who faced her begging for mercy.

She was ready.

The lintel creaked and a fine shower of plaster rained down on Benjamin. No, not rats, he decided. These feet were far too heavy, too slow. *But if not rats, then what?*

Benjamin shot out of bed. There was someone on the roof. He dismissed the thought as impossible and yet, as he listened, there it was again: the definite sound of a human foot on the tiles.

Careful so as not to disturb his father, Ben made his way to the window which jutted out of the sloping roof of their attic room. He rubbed the glass but he couldn't see anything through the spider's web of ice and his lip curled back in frustration. Above him the roof groaned again as a body adjusted its balance, shifting weight from one foot to another. It couldn't be a burglar, he reasoned;

they had less than nothing and none of that was worth stealing. There was only one answer: the Weeping Man had found him already.

Ben's first instinct was to run. To wake Pa and Nathaniel and then all of them could leg it. But then he remembered Molly Marbank and his sense of shame came back to haunt him. His hands began to rage within, throbbing with the same invisible power that had nearly shot Jago Moon out of his chair.

A sudden anger took hold of him, bigger than his fear, bigger than the danger. He had unfinished business with the Weeping Man. And if he couldn't handle him on his own, then there were two more Kingdoms in the room – surely they could manage him together?

The sash window was frozen shut, and Ben began to hammer against it with his palms, desperately trying to force it upwards.

Come on then!

A terrible banging was coming from below Lucy's feet. For some reason best known to himself, Ben Kingdom was trying to open a window that had been frozen shut. The noise echoed across the street and Lucy winced. She had been sent here to watch over him and make sure that he didn't draw attention to himself. *He might just as well shout "Here I am, come and get me!"* she thought. *He really doesn't have a clue what he's facing.*

Whether Ben Kingdom was the Hand or not, it was vital that the Legion didn't get their claws into him. They feared the Hand of Heaven more than they feared the might of the British Army, and if they even suspected that this scruffy East End kid might be the one who would bring about their downfall, they would stamp out his life without a second thought.

Lucy glanced down into the street and saw Jago Moon signalling to her. She read his hand gestures: *Two Legionnaires, advancing fast from the river end of the street.*

Shut up, Ben! she thought with increasing annoyance, as in the room beneath her the last hope for the Watchers continued to struggle with the simple task of opening a window. Quickly, Lucy skidded down the slope of tiles until she was balanced on the guttering, where she could get a better look at her enemy. Moon was right; she could see the disturbance in the snow around the manhole cover where they had emerged from the sewers like the rats they were. Two sets of tracks leading into the shadows.

Lucy liked Mr. Moon. He was fierce. He was strict. He terrified the younger ones and he enjoyed nothing better than a good fight. In many ways, he reminded Lucy of herself.

She stood poised, the wind tossing her long blonde hair around her slender face, waiting for the order from Moon to either hold her ground or move forward to engage.

Attack! signalled Moon and Lucy felt the rush of adrenaline as she sprinted across the rooftop; as nimble as a cat, and more than happy to use her claws.

Ben's pounding became more insistent, his hands throbbing with inner fire.

His brother Nathaniel started to stir.

His father was rousing.

The window gave way to a final push, and Arctic wind filled the room, bringing with it a swarm of snowflakes like angry wasps. Benjamin ignored their icy stings as he scrambled his way up onto the windowsill.

"What do you think you're doing?" Jonas Kingdom mumbled, groggy with sleep.

Ben didn't have time to answer; he had his feet on the window ledge, his arms bracing himself in the frame. He had to see.

Craning his neck, he caught a flurry of movement behind and above him. For a fraction of a second, Ben made out a figure standing beside the chimney pot. Then it was gone, running along the ridge of the roof with remarkable agility, before dropping down onto a lower roof and out of sight.

Inside the room his father and brother were both grumbling at him.

Ben sighed in resignation. As always he had some explaining to do.

The Legion scouts realized they had been spotted.

As soon as Jago Moon started to *tap tap tap* down the Lane towards them with his cane, Captain Mickelwhite knew it was their signal to leave. At his side, John Bedlam cracked his knuckles and made to rush the old man, but Mickelwhite reined him in with a firm hand on his shoulder.

"Steady, John," said Mickelwhite, dragging him back under cover. "We choose our fights, remember? Strike when *we* are ready, hit hard when we know we can win," he reasoned at a whisper.

"Yeah, well I'm ready now," snarled Bedlam. "It's about time that annoying old geezer got what was comin' to him."

Mickelwhite controlled his own emotions, since his partner was clearly incapable of controlling his. He pointed upwards and Bedlam followed his gaze. The other Watcher was on the move as well, almost dancing across the roof towards them.

"It's Scarface," hissed Bedlam, catching sight of the livid wound that split the girl's face in two.

"Come on," urged Mickelwhite, heading back towards the manhole and the safety of the sewers. "We need to report in."

"Another time then, beautiful," Bedlam whispered to himself with a final lingering look at the Watcher girl. Then he dragged the metal cover back into place over their heads, locked it tight, and they both descended the ladder into the hidden world of the Legion; down into the Under.

"Benjamin!" Jonas Kingdom barked, slamming the window and shutting out the storm. "What the hell are you playing at, boy? Some of us have got to work in a few hours."

Nathaniel gave him a look that was part smile, part pity, and then rolled over, his back to him. Jonas returned to his own bed and in minutes the pair of them were snoring again.

Ben stayed awake. He listened for footfalls on the roof. He listened for noises in the street. But the only thing that he could hear was the echo of his father's words.

Although he loved his father, there were times when he could almost hate him too; hate the injustice of it. All his life, he had felt as if he were being punished for a crime that he didn't commit.

It had never been spoken out loud, but Ben saw it in his father's eyes, felt it in the tone of his voice. *You murdered her, Ben. We'd be a happy family if it wasn't for you.*

He missed her too, didn't they understand that?

He hadn't killed her. It wasn't his fault.

How did they think he felt? Knowing that his mother gave her life to bring him into the world.

DAY TWO
21ST DECEMBER, 1891

CHAPTER 9

THE FEATHERED MEN

The Feathered Men were restless. Their screeching echoed through the tunnels of the Under, a shrill and angry conversation in a language no human ear should hear.

Claw Carter watched them cautiously. He had stalked tigers and the rules were much the same: move slowly, move silently. Try not to reek of fear.

There were hundreds of hidden chambers in the subterranean world of the Under, the secret realm of tunnels and catacombs that the Legion called home, but none were as dreaded as the nesting pens where the Feathered Men took their rest. Few dared to approach unless they were under strict orders, and then only reluctantly. Claw Carter, however, was not like other men.

The Feathered Men were remarkable creatures: part man, part bird; all evil. Carter admired them, admired their simplicity. They were killing machines, nothing more. Looking at them, it was hard to imagine that once they had been angelic beings, members of the high order of the Seraphim, whose sole purpose was to sing the praises of their Creator. But that had been a long time ago, before the rebellion in Heaven, Carter reminded himself. A lot had happened since then. The uprising had failed and the once majestic Feathered Men had been cast out with all the other rebel angels; hurled down into the depths of the Pit. Far, far away from Heaven's light.

In a way, the Feathered Men had never stopped falling, Carter thought, as he watched them. It was as if their hearts were set on descending lower and lower into depravity and greed. One at a time, they had been summoned by the Legion down the centuries, through sacrifice, ritual and blood. Lots of blood. And now they did the Legion's bidding, if it suited them. The relationship between the Feathered Men and the Legion was not an easy one, Carter knew, neither side having much to offer in the way of trust. But it worked because of a shared vision: they both wanted revenge on the One who had rejected them.

Carter observed the Feathered Men as they roosted in the eaves, squatting on the beams high overhead, gripping tight with their strangely elongated hands and feet. They did not require much in the way of comfort: a vaulted ceiling where they could take their rest, straw to defecate in, fresh meat to eat. A sconce of tallow candles flickered in the corner nearest to the stout oak doors, providing just enough light to cast the nesting chamber into shadows. These ageless, immortal creatures disliked the light; perhaps it reminded them too much of the life they had left behind, Carter mused.

Every now and then a squabble would erupt and they lashed out spitefully, snapping with their beaks and raking their talons across each other's flesh until the dispute was resolved. They were kindred spirits, Carter thought; they did what they wanted, took what they desired. *Much like myself.*

And although they were monstrous in appearance, like Carter with his claw, the Feathered Men were spiritual beings too; they understood the invisible things of this world. They understood the nature of the Coin. That was why he was here now.

Although he was not in the habit of explaining his

plans to anyone, he continued to be amazed that even someone as intelligent as Ruby Johnson failed to grasp the significance of the Coins. *Thirty pieces of silver*; wasn't it obvious? Didn't everyone know the story of Judas, the man who betrayed Jesus for a purse of Roman coins?

The Coins of Blood.

For nearly two thousand years they had brought out the worst in men, whispering to them in the secret hours of the night, enticing them to yield to the evil lurking inside their own hearts. The Watchers had tried to hide them, of course, scattering them around the world and locking them away. Tried and failed. Carter smiled; such naivety. The Watchers would never understand that greed would always win in the end.

As far as he understood, the great power of the Coins was that they freed a man to do the unthinkable. To hold just one of the Coins in your hand was to break the last chains of morality that kept you bound. They encouraged you to give in to your darkest urges, to do whatever you desired without a care for the consequences. To become totally free.

Free to kill Mr. Sweet, for example. Free to wipe out the Council of Seven and install yourself as supreme ruler of the Legion.

Carter had grown to despise the Seven. They were weak, insipid. They had amassed twenty-nine of the Judas Coins but they lacked the courage or the imagination to do anything with them except to shut them away in the dark. True, they might be working on some grand plan from which he was excluded, but whatever their scheme was, it was taking far too long for Carter's liking; he was a man of action. No, he was decided. When the last Coin was his, he would make his move.

The last Coin was the key. Each of the thirty held some power, but the thirtieth was the most potent, the most corrupting. Twenty-nine coins had not been enough to turn Judas from good to evil. But thirty…that was enough to unleash Hell.

And that was precisely what Carter intended to do.

But the Coin had eluded him. So far.

The Feathered Men would aid him, he knew, just as they had done in the past. The Council of Seven had decreed that the Feathered Men were only to be released from the holding pens with their express permission, but Claw Carter wasn't really in the business of seeking approval from anyone. No one understood the Feathered Men like he did; no one else fully appreciated their needs. Many was the time that he had let them fly free on an errand for him. All they needed was the right motivation.

As if on cue, there was a tentative knock on the doors and two trembling youths appeared, leading a cow. The cow was blindfolded, out of necessity. It would panic if it saw the Feathered Men. Just as the two boys were doing now.

They left gratefully, only too happy to close the door behind them and run. They did not see Carter guide the poor animal into the middle of the nesting chamber. They didn't see the expression on his face as he ran his claw along the cow's belly and then, in one swift slash, ripped her open from gullet to groin, spilling her steaming entrails onto the floor. But they could hear the terrible ecstasy of the Feathered Men as they feasted.

"Breakfast!" Carter declared. "Come and get it!"

Ben looked into his bowl. Porridge; at least that's how Mrs. McLennon described it. It was actually a sticky, grey sludge with more than a hint of sawdust. Although that didn't stop all of her tenants from gobbling it up, the adults around the kitchen table, the children and infants scattered across the floor. Except for the slurping, it was a moment of happy silence. Even the Vineys didn't row over breakfast.

Ben looked at his father across the table, hoping for

some sign that he had been forgiven for the disturbance the night before. Jonas Kingdom gave him a quick smile, and Ben knew that their relationship, such as it was, had been restored.

Ben lifted his bowl to his mouth and licked it clean with his tongue. Satisfied that he hadn't missed a solitary scrap, he wiped his lips with the back of his hand and then flashed his most dazzling smile at the O'Rourke girls.

They did not respond.

Mrs. McLennon started to gather up the empty bowls and they all understood that it was time for them to leave. There were never any seconds, so no one asked.

When she took his bowl, Mr. Wachowski belched appreciatively and scratched at a morsel that was nesting in his beard. "Kind lady," he said.

"Och, no," Mrs. McLennon demurred. "Nothing but my Christian duty."

They all paid extra in their rent for the "Christian duty", but again no one said a word.

"That was splendid, Mrs. McLennon," said Jonas, rising from the table. "Come on then, son, we don't want to be getting under Mrs. Mac's feet."

Nathaniel Kingdom rose swiftly. "Yes, Pa," he said, ready for a day working at his father's side.

Benjamin Kingdom stood more slowly and didn't say a word.

Stiff and cold, Ruby Johnson awoke to find herself on the cellar floor in the Punch and Judy. Rolling the numbness from her shoulders, she scanned the ground until she found the coin that had thrown Professor Carter into such a rage the night before. She picked it up, balanced it on her thumb and flicked it into the air, catching it neatly and then tucking it in her pocket. If Carter didn't want it then she was sure that someone else would pay her handsomely; failing that she could spend it herself. She placed it between her teeth and bit. Real silver too. She didn't understand what all the fuss was about. Boys could be so silly sometimes.

Ruby left the Punch and Judy as quietly as she had arrived and set off in search of some breakfast. *Eggs would be nice today,* she thought, or *a bit of bacon. Where can I acquire them?* she wondered.

Although she would never confess it, Ruby was still irked that she had shown herself up. She had dragged Carter out on a wild goose chase. She had, in short, failed him, and that wasn't her style at all. The mysterious Coin was clearly far more important to Carter than she had realized and if anyone was going to find it, she was determined that it would be her. Her talents deserved recognition.

Besides, not all of the others in the organization to which she belonged possessed her social graces. Rewards and honour would be wasted on them, in her opinion. Some members of the Legion, she had to admit, were not pleasant people at all.

And if the thugs and bully boys didn't get their grubby fingers on the Coin, then the Feathered Men surely would. She shuddered at the thought. She wouldn't want to receive a visit from the Feathered Men for all the money in the world.

CHAPTER 10

A BIT OF LUCK

Back in their room, the three Kingdom men got ready for their day; two as dockers, one as an apprentice cooper and sometime mudlark. Ben didn't mind learning the trade of barrel-making. He didn't really mind mudlarking either, searching for things he might sell that had fallen into the filthy banks of the Thames. Although he was less than happy that the very best pickings were always to be found in the deep mud around the gratings, where the sewers flowed into the river. But what made him unhappy was that his father never asked him to work in the docks at his side.

Jonas Kingdom was a good man, everyone said so.

The salt of the earth. Ben could easily see why his mother had fallen in love with him; in spite of everything that was harsh about their lives there was always a sparkle in his eyes.

Today his father's eyes were positively ablaze.

"Can you show Ben, Pa?" Nathaniel spoke and Ben snapped out of his daze.

Jonas threw a silent glance in Ben's direction and then, with no further hesitation, drew something from inside his jacket.

"Just quick," said Jonas. "Then we need to get this little beauty tucked away somewhere safe."

Both boys drew close and watched as their father unfolded a square of dark cloth, like a magician performing a trick. Nestled in the velvet was a single silver coin. It was small and old, and not very much to look at, and yet as Ben gazed upon it, he was filled with a yearning that he had never known before. He reached out to touch it, but his father snatched it away. "It's not for touching," he said, "it's for buying us a better life."

"How did you get it?" asked Ben.

Again, Nathaniel and Jonas shared a glance.

"It was the strangest thing," said Nathaniel. "Can I tell him, Pa?" Jonas nodded. "There was this 'Jyptian fellow," Nathaniel began, "dressed in these long robes and a turban. We get all sorts down at the docks, don't we, Pa?" Another nod. "Anyway, he was acting all peculiar, walking back and forth and waving his arms like he was arguing with someone, 'cept he was the only one there. He looked old, as if his face had been all dried up by the sun, and there was something else about him too, wasn't there, Pa?"

"The man was scared," said Jonas, taking over the tale. "I went over to him and introduced myself, to see if he was in trouble, anything I could do, and he gave me this look – it sent a shiver right through me. It was as if he was in prison and I was the first light he had seen in years."

Jonas's expression became distant, as if he was remembering something he would rather forget. Then he continued. "He grabbed my wrist. His hands were as bony as claws, although I don't think I could have broken his hold if I'd wanted to." He shook his head slightly, as if trying to shake off the memory of that skeletal grip. "Then he forced the coin into my palm. 'Take it,' he said. 'Take it and destroy it.' And then he ran away."

"Ran like the bobbies were after him," laughed Nathaniel.

"Why would he want you to destroy it?" asked Ben, incredulous.

"Perhaps he wasn't right in the head," Jonas suggested,

forcing a laugh as if to chase his own doubts away. "Don't suppose we'll ever know his half of it. And truth be told, it doesn't matter, because for once a bit of luck has landed in our laps."

All three of them gazed at the small circle of silver; the miracle in their midst. "I could take it if you like," suggested Ben eagerly, breaking the silence. "I'm sure Professor Carter would be able to tell me all about it. He could even give us an idea of how much it might be worth—"

"Right before he took it away and put it in a case in that blasted museum." Jonas shook his head in disbelief. "I just don't get you sometimes," he told Ben. "You act like you're so full of learning, yet you don't do much thinking." He paused to let his words sink in. "Do you think anyone else is going to believe for one minute that some Egyptian geezer just gave us this coin? Don't you think that Carter will start asking questions that we don't have the answers to?" He closed his fist around the coin to display his resolve. "No, Ben, my mind's made up. Your precious professor is just the same as the rest of them. He'd take this coin off us and keep it for himself."

Ben wanted to protest. Professor Carter was not like that. *He's a good man,* Ben thought, *like you.*

Instead, he held his tongue.

"This coin isn't going anywhere, you understand?" said Jonas. "Not until I've had proper time to think on how best we can use it." Nathaniel showed his agreement by nodding hard. "In the meantime, we've got to keep it out of the way of prying eyes and sticky fingers."

Jonas turned to Ben. "Make yourself useful, lad, and go and keep watch on the stairs. Sing out if you see anyone. I need to get this treasure buried."

CHAPTER 11

POISON
TO THE SOUL

The man was not from Egypt as Jonas Kingdom had assumed. His name was Nazir el Hussain and before he became a murderer he was once a prince of Persia.

None of his subjects would recognize him if they saw him now. His robes had lost their lustre, and his face, which some had called the most handsome in all of Arabia, was haunted and gaunt. He was old before his time.

Nazir looked at his hands and wondered when they had wasted away to skin and bone. They were trembling and he understood why. He was shaking with need. Since he had given the Coin away it was as if he was burning up from the inside.

He wanted it back so terribly.

A year ago, when he first saw the Coin, it had belonged to another man who was as consumed by its power and beauty as he had become. He would never forget the surprise on the old man's face when he had pushed the dagger into his chest, or the sound of the aged fingers snapping as he broke their dying grip.

"The Coin is mine; you shall not have it," his father had said with his final breath.

It was poison to the soul, Nazir understood that now. That was why he had to put as much distance between himself and the Coin as possible, if he was to have a chance to be free. Since he had given the Coin to that poor fool at the docks, Nazir had not stopped running. Or looking over his shoulder.

That same day he took passage on the first ship that would carry him, not caring which shore it was headed for. He paid the captain too much and, as soon as the deal was struck, he wasted no time in getting below decks. His only plan was to stay hidden in his cabin with the door locked until an ocean separated him from that merciless piece of silver.

Nazir turned the key in the lock and then sank to the floor, with his back against the door. It was cool and dark in his cramped cabin and a wooden shutter across the single porthole easily held back the feeble daylight. Perhaps if he could survive the voyage, endure the ceaseless pull of the Coin until he was totally beyond its reach, then he might have a chance to live again. Not that he deserved it, his conscience told him.

It was only then that he realized he was not alone. There were other shapes in the darkness.

His eyes strained against the dim light until they rested on a huddle of lean bodies in the far corner. *Hashshashin*, he thought; assassins come too late to steal the Coin. But the more he looked, the more he knew these were not mere *men* sent to kill him. Their limbs were disturbingly disproportionate; slightly too narrow, slightly too long. Fingers with nails as sharp and hard as bone. He could see their strong, wiry frames and naked skin which looked as if it had been stretched too tight over elongated muscles.

Things with the forms of men but with the heads and wings of eagles.

His religion taught him that demons were real. And Nazir el Hussain understood instantly why these ones had come for him.

"The Coin," one of them hissed at him, its voice an ugly croak. "Where is the Coin?"

Nazir spread his arms and showed them his empty palms.

Another of the creatures opened its beak and issued a harsh shriek. They observed Nazir for one more second and then fell on him as one; a sudden rush of talons and feathers as black as the night.

"The Coin!" they screamed. "Where is the Coin?"

Nazir el Hussain did not resist the embrace of the Feathered Men, not even as they ripped his flesh and began to feast on his body. For a minute he lay twitching on the floor as his soft innards gave way to the rampage of their beaks.

"Kingdom," he said at last. Then he twitched no more.

Perhaps death would bring him the peace that he longed for.

"Anyone about?" asked Jonas Kingdom.

"Not that I can see, Pa," Ben replied from his lookout post in their bedroom doorway. He was watching the landing to make sure that Mrs. Mac or any of the other residents didn't come upstairs to pay them an unexpected call.

Satisfied that they were alone, Jonas rolled back his mattress and set about gently loosening a short piece of floorboard, rocking it back and forth until it quietly came free in his hand. This was where the Kingdoms hid their wealth, such as it was, amid the dust and the mouse droppings. At the last count, their combined savings amounted to two shillings and eleven pence: the price of a new pair of boots, although none of them imagined that the money would be squandered on such a luxury.

This Coin would turn their fortunes around, his father was right about that.

Although he was meant to be watching the stairs, Ben's eyes never left the Coin. Not for a second. He had never seen anything so fascinating before.

And it was then that he decided he would take it to Professor Carter anyway.

Where was the harm in that?

CHAPTER 12

GREY WING

The Feathered Men were always at their most passive when they had finished gorging. Now Carter spoke with them, if not as their friend, then at least not as their prey.

Carter had accumulated a great many languages in his travels; he was fluent in Mongolian, Russian, Swahili, Mandarin, Gujarati and many obscure tribal dialects, as well as the French, Spanish, German and Portuguese of the less adventurous traveller. Often he found that his claw could speak louder than words, but sometimes a more subtle message needed to be conveyed.

The language of the Feathered Men was ugly on the tongue, all clicks and soft palette noises, interspersed with shrill shrieks. It was not a rich idiom, it lacked beauty and rhythm; although it did contain forty-five different words for killing, Carter noted. Most importantly, by learning it, Carter had made himself the only one who could communicate with these fallen Seraphim in their own language. A vital persuasive skill if you wanted to employ them as your own private army.

A large Feathered Man, whose battered wings had grown steel-grey with age, barged his way to the front of the flock, asserting his status as leader. Carter ignored the blood that dripped from Grey Wing's battle-scarred beak and the two conversed, while all around them the chamber echoed with the noise of bones being gnawed.

"The missing Coin," said Carter.

Grey Wing observed him coldly, his eagle head tilted to one side. "The search continues," the Feathered Man replied.

"And?" said Carter, with some frustration.

"And?" Grey Wing mimicked.

It was often this way; Grey Wing was the most capricious of a spiteful breed.

For a fleeting second, Carter appeared downcast. Grey Wing squatted on his haunches and regarded him mockingly. Then, in a single fluid movement, Carter stepped in tight, grabbing the feathers on the back of Grey

Wing's skull and yanking his head backwards until the soft tissue of his neck was exposed to the tip of Carter's claw.

Overhead, the other Feathered Men screamed; some in anger, others in cruel delight.

"You need me more than I need you," Carter hissed. "Don't you ever forget it!" He allowed his claw to draw blood and saw alarm in those huge yellow eyes. "Mr. Sweet and the Council of Seven will keep you locked down here for ever. Is that what you want? To rot? But help me find the Coin, and I will usher in a new day for the Legion. No more interminable plans that come to nothing, no more skulking around in the shadows, but open war on the streets of London. And you, my fine feathered friend, will rule the skies, and dine on anyone you choose!"

Gradually, Carter relinquished his grip as he felt Grey Wing's acquiescence. When he was released, the Feathered Man staggered back, making a gagging noise. Grey Wing brought his hand to his throat and it came away bloody. He considered that for a moment and then resumed his squatting position, unfurling his great dark wings and wrapping them around himself like a cloak.

"There was a man, yesterday, at the docks," Grey Wing began.

"Go on."

"He was a Coin carrier."

"You're certain?"

Grey Wing nodded. "There is no mistaking the scent of a man entirely given over to evil."

"And?"

"We found him in his hiding place and he danced a merry dance with us."

"You mean you tormented and ate him," Carter offered.

Grey Wing made a repulsive noise which Carter took to be laughter.

"He was a scrawny thing," said Grey Wing. "All bone and gristle."

"And the Coin?" Carter prompted.

"He no longer had it, he had passed it on to another."

"But you can track it, sniff them out?"

"No," said Grey Wing. "The Coins don't consume a man instantly; some men don't yield to their influence at all. It's all down to choice, as you well know, Professor Carter. It's not compulsory to yield to temptation."

"So we are no closer to finding it." Carter could feel his anger growing.

Grey Wing allowed the silence to stretch between them; with his beak for a mouth, it was impossible to tell whether he was smiling.

"We have a name," said Grey Wing finally. "The Coin is now in the hands of someone named 'Kingdom'."

Carter was jubilant. "Then I have one last thing to say to you," he said, standing aside to allow Grey Wing a glimpse of the open door. "Fetch!"

It was strangely heavy for such a little thing.

Ben cupped the Coin in his hand and was struck by the uneasy thought that if he fell into the Thames with it in his grasp, it would drag him down to the bottom, never to surface again.

He had waited for his father and brother to leave for the docks, watching from the window until they were both out of sight before he made his move. And now the Coin was his. He didn't feel comfortable going behind his father's back; but he was only taking the Coin for Professor Carter to have a look at, he reassured himself. He was not stealing it; that was important. He was *borrowing* it.

He often took things up to the museum that he found when he was mudlarking: bits of pottery, hatpins, lost brooches, old coins, all left in the silt of the river and dredged up by scruffy urchins like him. He had never found anything really valuable, more's the pity, but over the years he liked to think that he had struck up a friendship with Professor Carter. "Bring me what you find, my boy," the man would say. "Particularly any old coins you discover."

It was all very clear to Ben when he ran through the scenario in his mind. Carter would be delighted to see him and would declare the Coin to be an amazing find, a real treasure. Then, after a special ceremony, at which the Kingdom family would be guests of honour, the Coin would take pride of place in the British Museum and people would come from miles around to gaze upon it. Finally, Her Majesty Queen Victoria would be so grateful that she would reward Jonas Kingdom for his services to the Empire, and in his quiet and modest way, his father would become a man of means and no longer have to break his back for the price of stale bread. That was how Ben saw it, anyway. His pa was going to be so pleased with him.

Buoyed up on these thoughts, Ben was bounding down the stairs three at a time and didn't see Mr. Wachowski occupying his usual step at the bottom until he was stumbling over him. Ben fell forwards clumsily, his hands slapping onto the hard tiles just in time to stop him from breaking his nose. Mr. Wachowski groaned with the impact, holding his back in pain. And the Coin slipped from Ben's grasp and went rolling across the floor.

They both forgot their injuries and instead watched the Coin, mesmerized. A single coin, spinning like a ballerina; more fascinating and alluring than any dancer who ever graced the stage.

Slowly, the Coin stopped its dance and then toppled flat onto the cold tiles.

Neither of them spoke.

"What's this, Ben Kingdom?" said Mr. Wachowski, reaching out with a podgy hand. "You're a rich man?"

Ben's left hand flashed out and snatched the Coin away before the Polish man could touch it. "Watch carefully," said Ben, holding it up before the man's eyes and passing it back and forth. Then, just like the street conjurer he had learned the trick from in the first place, Ben rolled his knuckles and made the Coin tumble from finger to finger across the back of his hand, before making it disappear completely, ending his routine with a theatrical clap.

"Which hand?" he asked the confused man, holding out two fists for him to choose from. After a moment of deliberation, Mr. Wachowski picked the left. With his flair for the dramatic Ben opened his fingers with agonizing slowness to reveal an empty palm. He then puzzled the man even further by opening his right hand and showing that to be empty too.

"What's this, Mr. Wachowski?" said Ben, mimicking the man's favourite phrase. And as Mr. Wachowski sat dumbfounded, Ben reached into the tobacco pouch that was a permanent resident on the man's lap, and retrieved the Coin from within.

"Bravo!" declared the old man, clapping joyfully.

"Right, I'm going to hook it," said Ben. And with a cheeky grin on his face and the Coin deep in his pocket, he opened the front door and left.

Outside, the feet of men and horses had turned the snow to slush. Above him the sky was a sheet of cloud the colour of bad milk. More snow was coming.

He set off at a breakneck pace that quickly ate up the ground. Ben knew that if he turned up late for work, his master would have a nice warm beating waiting for his backside; Mr. Smutts was a generous man like that. In his haste, he almost didn't register a shape standing motionless in the alleyway opposite his front door: the shape of an old man, with gnarled hands twisted around a white cane, and a battered case at his side. Jago Moon, the blind bookseller.

Moon didn't call out or signal to Benjamin in any way, and yet Ben could feel the cloudy spheres of his blind eyes burning into his back all the way down the Lane.

✳

Of course, Carter knew that it was all rather hit or miss. There had to be dozens of Kingdoms in London, possibly hundreds. It was quite likely that a lot of innocent people would get hurt before the Feathered Men found the right one. War was like that unfortunately; civilians got wounded all the time.

Kingdom... The name rang a bell from somewhere. Was one of those guttersnipes that he employed to trawl the sewers called Kingdom? He tried to put a face to the name as he made his way down the tunnel that would take him to his rooms in the basement of the British Museum. He had to keep up the day job; for now.

"Knight Commander Carter, sir!" a voice called behind him and he turned to see a young Legionnaire rushing to report. The boy came to a stop in front of him and stood ramrod straight, his left fist clenched to his breast in salute.

"Busy night, Captain Mickelwhite?"

"Yes, sir, we almost had a run-in with Jago Moon, sir."

Carter could feel his interest waning already.

"He and another Watcher were guarding a boy on Old Gravel Lane."

Carter nodded and began to move on again. "Good, good," he said dismissively.

"We asked around and we were able to find out the

boy's name, sir," Mickelwhite called at his retreating back. "Ben Kingdom."

Claw Carter halted in his tracks. He believed in many things, but not coincidences.

CHAPTER 13

MONSTERS

Ben was almost twenty minutes late.

He was going to be in trouble. Mr. Smutts would take the belt from round his waist and Ben was going to taste its lick right across his backside. He thought of the Coin in his pocket, so hot and heavy, and didn't think one small beating was too big a price to pay.

However, as it turned out, being late was the least of his worries.

When Ben turned the corner of the Lane towards the cooper's, he ploughed straight into a solid wall of bodies. Old Gravel Lane was often a crush, but this took the biscuit, Ben thought. The throng was so thick that he could barely shoulder his way between them. The most unusual thing about the crowd was that they weren't going anywhere; they were just stood there, gawping at something, and muttering. And there was a strange tang in the air that was beginning to scratch at Ben's nose. He barged his way through the crowd, his ears pricked as he made out snatches of conversation.

"*Ain't it terrible.*"

"*Someone should do somefink.*"

"*Oh my gawd, they're all gonna perish.*"

"Let me through," Ben gasped, using his elbows to fight his passage through the pack. "Have a bit of mercy and let me through!"

With a last desperate push, Ben finally emerged in front of the cooper's and it was then that he understood. In the place where Mr. Smutts's workshop used to stand, Ben was greeted by an inferno. The flames were having their way with the old wooden building, raging without thought or compassion, consuming whatever they chose. In the distance, Ben could hear the bell of the fire wagon, and even as he urged it on, he already knew in his heart that it was too late. It was winter in London. All the water was as hard as bricks. What were they going to do, throw snowballs at the blaze?

"What's the matter with you people?" Ben screamed,

already feeling the heat licking at his face. "Why don't you help?" Squinting against the sting of the smoke, Ben searched for two figures in the haze: Old Man Smutts and his son, Stanley.

"Mr. Smutts!" Ben shouted. He went as close as he dared, hot splinters raining down on him as the workshop began to groan with the effort of standing. "Mr. Smutts! Stan!"

A figure staggered from the mouth of the blaze, through the ring of fire that marked where the door had once been, and then fell face down. Ben ran to him and turned him over, cradling his head in his lap. It was a boy, about his own age, the skin on his hands red and blistered where he had tried to protect his face.

"Stan, listen to me, you're going to be alright," said Ben, scooping up handfuls of sooty slush and rubbing them across the boy's burned hands. "Is your father safe? I haven't seen him."

Stanley's eyes opened wide and looked back at the blazing building, salt tears drawing lines down his blackened cheeks. "Pa," he said.

The fire brigade had finally appeared at the end of the street and almost grudgingly the crowd began to admit their wagon and horses. But Ben didn't have time to wait for them to act. Nor did Mr. Smutts.

Quickly, Ben whipped off his jacket and began to roll it in the slush. When it was wet through, he shoved his arms back into the sleeves and, hunching his shoulders, pulled his jacket up over his head, hat and all. With his face pushed into the crook of his arm, he made for the door.

Standing there on the edge of Hell, with only the flames before him, he paused. "I'll bring him back for you, Stan," he said.

Ben knew that it was a bad idea as soon as he stepped inside. A cooper's shop was not a good place to be in a fire. Planks of wood stored out the back. Fresh wooden barrels stacked floor to ceiling. Wooden roof supported by wooden beams. Wooden frame around the small windows. Wooden frame around the wooden door. Carpet of wood shavings on the floor. One thing Ben knew about wood: it doesn't half burn.

Pretty much as soon as he entered the building, Ben was convinced that he was going to burn with it.

Steam was already rising from his sodden jacket and his boots were beginning to smoulder beneath his feet. It was as if he had stepped inside a furnace: all that he could see was flames. Beautiful, rampant, hungry flames.

"Mr. Smutts!" he shouted, edging his way towards the

back of the shop, squinting to see through slitted eyes. The air around him was alive with sparks where the sawdust was igniting in flight. Ben's words were lost against the roar of the inferno, and his lungs were filled with heavy smoke that threatened to drag him to his knees. Ben coughed until his guts ached, but he dared not give in to it; he knew too well that if he let the fire take hold of him, it would never let him go.

Above his head the rafters gave an ominous groan and released a shower of sparks and cinders that fell onto the shield of his sodden coat like molten rain. The fire was so hot now that the iron hoops on the barrels were beginning to burst and the rivets that had been hammered so carefully into place were exploding from their sockets. Ben could smell his own hair beginning to catch.

Through the hole of the doorway and the clouds of smoke, he could just about make out the shapes of the firemen outside, shouting and barking their orders and not rescuing him from the blaze. Ben dropped to his knees as a chunk of ceiling detached itself and came crashing to the ground behind him while he sheltered beneath the remains of his coat. The smoke was so thick that he couldn't tell one direction from another. Each breath sucked more pain into his lungs. His exposed hands were raw, the floorboards beneath his knees burning yet more holes in his trousers, seeking out the soft flesh inside.

And there's you thinking you might freeze to death this winter, he thought wryly as the window exploded outwards, showering firemen and gawpers alike with razor-edged splinters of glass.

With a final effort, Ben pushed on through the firestorm and out to the back of the workshop, where the flames had not yet completely taken hold. He quickly saw that a large beam had fallen from the roof and lay heavily across a man's legs, pinning him down. Kneeling beside the prone body, Ben saw thick blood soaking through the trousers and a terrible stump of white bone. Mr. Smutts's face was grey, his eyes shut. His chest was still.

"NO!" shouted Ben. He took his employer by the shoulders and began to shake him. "No!" he said firmly. "You're not dead."

"And I'm not deaf either," said Mr. Smutts, and they shared a moment like none that had passed between them before.

Mr. Smutts smiled at Ben and touched a hand to his cheek. "You're late, Master Kingdom," he said gently, wincing through his pain. "Is this any way to treat your master?"

"Sack me later," said Ben.

✳

Even when he thought about it afterwards, Ben couldn't explain how he shifted the beam from Mr. Smutts's broken leg, or how he managed to drag the man from the burning building. It was as if he had found a well of energy inside himself that he never knew existed.

He remembered the strange throbbing sensation in his right hand though, along his whole arm in fact, and the feeling that he was somehow much stronger than he had ever been before. Strong enough to lift a burning rafter, strong enough to carry a full grown man to safety. *And he's quite a fat bloke too*, thought Ben to himself proudly. *I don't know me own strength.*

Exhausted, Ben lay down in the snow beside his employer, gasping for a breath of air that wasn't poisoned with smoke.

Stanley crawled over to his father's side and the look they exchanged was all the reward that Ben could ask for. Then the cooper's shop collapsed in on itself in a mushroom cloud of flames and the true agony of Mr. Smutts's shattered leg began to really kick in.

Clenching his teeth, Mr. Smutts beckoned Ben closer with a twitch of his fingers. "Benjamin," he hissed.

Reluctantly, Ben obeyed. He didn't want any thanks, although a shilling wouldn't go amiss. "Really, Mr. Smutts, you don't have to—"

"Shut up and listen, Ben!" The voice was full of urgency.

Ben shut up and listened.

"They were looking for you, Benjamin. The ones who did this…" Mr. Smutts pointed to the cinders where his life's work once stood. "They were monsters, Benjamin. Demons." His eyes were wide as he spoke. "They were like men," he continued, "but with these huge wings, and their heads…" Smutts could hardly bring himself to say what he had seen. "Benjamin, they were an offence before God. As if some cruel boy had torn the head off a doll and sewn on a raven's head in its place." The haunted expression on Mr. Smutts's face gave Ben a hint of the nightmares the poor man would be suffering, long after his bones had mended.

"They spoke to me, if you could call it speaking; their accent was that thick. Would you believe it? Bird-men speaking the Queen's own English with their filthy tongues." He shook his head. "They said that they wanted Kingdom," Smutts continued and Ben's heart turned to lead inside his chest. "Well, I wouldn't tell 'em anything, told them to be off." Mr. Smutts tried a smile, but in vain.

"Then they grabbed Stanley, said that they would hurt him… I'm sorry, Benjamin. I had no choice." Mr. Smutts's eyes were filled with remorse. "I told them where you live."

Ben was on his feet and running even as the words sank home.

"Run, Benjamin," Mr. Smutts shouted from somewhere behind him. "Run!"

His blood roaring in his ears, Ben only had two thoughts as he pelted along. *Nathaniel*, he thought. *Pa!*

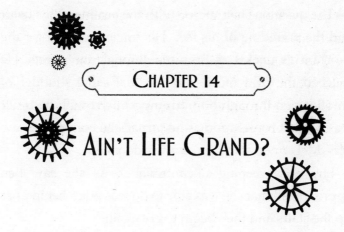

CHAPTER 14

AIN'T LIFE GRAND?

What if Pa and Nathaniel had gone back to their room? Would there be a monster with a bird's head waiting there to rip them apart?

Part of Ben considered running to Professor Carter for help. There was something about the man's fierce intelligence and even more fearsome claw that made most problems seem much smaller. But Ben's heart steered him straight towards home. Danger was looking for him. Last night it was in Skinners Lane and on the rooftops shrouded by snow, this morning it was waiting at the workshop in the flames.

Why was everyone suddenly out to get him?

The questions hammered with the beating of his heart and the pounding of his feet. His fingers reached for the Coin in his pocket as he raced through the streets. He touched the cold metal and felt that same shudder of emotion run through him; triumph mixed with desire. It was a small consolation as he turned the corner and saw Mrs. McLennon standing on their doorstep.

She was weeping uncontrollably. As she saw Ben approach, all that she was able to do was point behind her up the stairs and then begin to cry again.

Ben took the stairs two at a time, passing Mr. Wachowski in the hall, smoking and shaking his head. Mrs. O'Rourke stood watching through a crack in her door, the two smallest O'Rourkes gathered safely round her skirts; even Mrs. Viney had taken a rest from her screaming and was standing in her doorway, silent and pale.

He had no idea what he would do if he actually found someone waiting for him in his room. These people – he wasn't ready yet to believe Mr. Smutts's fantastic description of the bird-men – these *people* had already burned Mr. Smutts's workshop to the ground and they'd only escaped by the skin of their teeth. It was not a good plan to try to confront them single-handed, he knew that.

Pa, he thought, and he climbed the last few stairs

regardless of the danger that might be waiting for him at the top.

The bedroom door was shut and the lock appeared untouched. Ben put his ear to the wood and listened. There was nothing. Either the intruders had fled, or they were waiting patiently on the other side.

There was only one way to find out.

Ben chose to fling the door open with all his might, imagining that if there was someone lurking, there was a chance that the door would hit them and hit them hard. Instead, he found himself alone and face-to-face with destruction.

Everything that his family owned had been torn apart. The small table and chair had been reduced to firewood, the hiding place beneath the floorboards was now a gaping hole. Their clothes had been ransacked. The mattresses where his father and brother lay each night had been sliced open with knives. His own bed was in tatters, his secret books nothing more than strewn pages. Even his mother's Bible had been ripped to shreds.

It was no mystery how the culprits had got in: half the roof was lying on the floor. Ben looked through the ragged gap at the iron-hard sky. His visitor from the night before had obviously returned.

Well, ain't life grand? thought Ben.

✲

"I didn't see the scoundrels," said Mrs. McLennon when she joined Ben in the wreckage of his room. "But mark this, Moira McLennon will not be caught napping a second time." There was fire in her words and flint in her grey Scottish eyes, but Ben had no desire for this old woman to fight his battles for him.

There was nothing more for them to discuss.

Mrs. McLennon handed him a beef broth, which he received gratefully, and then after a moment of awkward silence she left him to it. "If there's anything else you're needing," she said, "I'll be in the kitchen."

Half-heartedly, Ben tried to bring some sort of order to the room. However, it didn't take long to realize that everything was too far gone to be rescued, and all that he had the energy to do was to re-stuff the mattresses as best he could and gather the rest of the debris to one side. Even that exhausted him, and he sat for a while with his back to the wall, hugging his knees. The one thing he did do was to put the pages of his mother's Bible together. It was a tiny book, so small that she might have carried it in her purse, and with print so dense that it made his eyes hurt. He placed a small kiss on the Bible's thumb-worn cover and imagined that in that breath he could smell his mother's perfume; a sigh of lemons and summer.

He tucked it back under his father's pillow, then he closed his eyes and tried not to think of anything at all.

When he awoke, the hole in the roof showed Ben that the day had raced away from him and the night would soon be drawing in. He put on his topcoat over the burned remains of his jacket, and settled his billycock hat on his head. It would be bitterly cold again tonight. Sitting on the remains of his mattress, he ran through a long list of questions and came up with no answers at all.

Ben still wanted to visit Professor Carter; he was convinced that the man might be able to shed some sort of light on this present darkness. That would have to wait though, because above all else Ben needed to be here when his father and brother returned. He had a vision of bird-men swooping down on them out of the sky, slashing at his family with sharp beaks and hands like talons.

He shook his head vigorously. *I've really got to stop reading such scary books*, he thought.

It was not unusual for Jonas and Nathaniel Kingdom to return home late. They would sometimes stop for a drink together at the Jolly Tar, which wasn't much to ask after a hard day's work. It was very unusual, however, for them to be out this late.

Ben had listened to the chimes of distant St George in the East ringing out first ten, then eleven and now twelve o'clock.

All was not well.

The moon was out and watching the city like an owl preparing to swoop. Ben couldn't shake the feeling that something terrible had happened to his family. The wickedness that had come looking for him at Mr. Smutts's was surely searching for them too. He stood in the window, watching and waiting. And shivering.

Then, from above his head, Ben heard the scrape of a boot against the tiles, and voices whispering, low and urgent.

Ben made a dash for the door. His own flurry of movement was matched by frantic activity overhead; there was no attempt to disguise the footsteps now.

Ben charged down the stairs, almost tripping over his own feet in the dark as he tried to put some distance between him and his pursuers. He plunged out of the front door and into the Lane. Looking back towards his small window, he could see two figures on his ruined roof, stark against the moonlit sky.

One of them was surprisingly small, Ben thought, probably not much older than him. It was the other one that scared him rigid. Ben recognized the silhouette and shuddered.

Even without seeing the tears on his cheeks or the sword beneath his coat, there was no mistaking the Weeping Man.

"Benjamin Kingdom!" called the Weeping Man, reaching out to him from the rooftop. "Come with me."

Before waiting for a reply, the Weeping Man's accomplice drew a crossbow from a shoulder holster and aimed it in Ben's direction.

Panic grabbed him tight. He looked around, uncertain which way to turn, but knowing that each second he delayed might cost him dearly. Then another voice hissed to him and his eyes were drawn to a gloved hand emerging from the shadows of a side alley.

"Oi, ginger! This way, if you fancy staying alive."

It was a pleasant voice, Ben thought. Certainly more reassuring than the one shouting at him from the roof.

The gloved hand spurred him on with a beckoning finger. Hugging the wall tight for cover, Ben ran over to find that the hand belonged to a girl with short, jagged hair and the most incredible eyes he had ever seen. It was the best surprise he had had in a long time.

She held out her hand to him and flashed her eyes.

Ben took her hand and ran.

It was all he seemed to do these days.

DAY THREE
22ND DECEMBER, 1891

Chapter 15

Hot Water

Ben felt exhilarated although he didn't quite know why. He expected that a lot of it had to do with the gloved hand that was holding his own, and the girl the hand belonged to. They were running for their lives in the midnight snow and all Ben could do was smile.

"Where are we going?" he asked as she pulled him through the backstreets, turning left, then right, then left again, ducking and weaving as they went.

"Hush," she said, but there was no anger in her voice.

Ben clasped her hand tighter and let her lead him on. High over their heads, they could hear voices and the rattle of boots on roof tiles, as each twist and turn they made on the ground was matched by their pursuers above. The street started to widen out, and as the girl dragged Ben onwards, he looked up to see the Weeping Man take a running leap from one side to the other.

He's never gonna make it, Ben thought...and then was proved wrong by the rattle of feet on the far side and a fine rain of tile fragments falling on his head.

"Who are those people?" he asked, impressed in spite of himself.

"Hush," she said again, her eyes sparkling like emeralds in the moonlight. She hauled him left and right through the maze of backstreets and then stopped at a wooden trapdoor.

"What's down there? Are we going to hide in a cellar?" Ben guessed.

The girl pushed him up against the wall then and pressed her finger to his lips. "Hush," she said. "Don't you ever stop asking questions?"

Ben felt very warm and he wasn't sure if it was because he had been running hell-for-leather or because he had never met anyone like this girl before. It took him a moment to realize that in fact the air itself was noticeably warmer here, and as he looked down he saw steam rising from the cellar door, carrying with it the harsh tang of carbolic.

Ben watched as the girl crouched and rapped on the hatch with her knuckles: two short knocks, then three long, then two short. Some sort of code, he supposed, and he was proved right when, after the rattling of bolts being drawn, an oriental face appeared from beneath the hatch.

With a furtive look left, right and skyward, the Chinese man beckoned them both into his underground lair. Ben clambered down the wooden steps behind the girl, while the man waited to bolt and lock the hatch behind them. No escape that way, thought Ben, and it occurred to him for the first time that he had put his life in the hands of this mysterious girl, based on her dazzling eyes and her smile alone.

Lucy Lambert scanned the streets below her in vain. The Kingdom boy was even more stupid than she had feared. One glimpse of a pretty face and he had run off with the Legion, hand in hand. *Damn him!*

She saw the Weeping Man walking towards her across the rooftop; they had split up in an effort to double their chances of getting to Ben. He still appeared to be at total peace, but Lucy couldn't stop the awful despondency that crashed down on her. She wandered to the edge of the roof and sat down heavily, her feet dangling in the empty air.

"I'm sorry," she said, not looking at the Weeping Man's face as he sat down beside her. "I'm so very sorry."

"You have nothing to apologize for," said the Weeping Man.

"But I do, don't I?" Lucy protested. "I was sent to guard him and I lost him. You know what the Legion is like; you know how twisted their ideas are. If Kingdom is taken in by their lies, you know what he will become."

The Weeping Man nodded but said nothing.

"He'll become the Hand of Hell!" Lucy was almost shouting with frustration. "He'll lead the Legion to victory and all this –" she flung out her own hands for emphasis – "this city, these people, will be destroyed." Tears brimmed in her one eye but she refused to let them fall. "Why didn't *you* stop him?" she challenged. "You could make him join us."

"Because it doesn't work that way," the Weeping Man replied gently. "We can never force anyone to join us; everyone has to choose for themselves."

"But Ben Kingdom is such an idiot!" Lucy protested.

"Have faith," said the Weeping Man. "He'll do the right thing."

The Chinese man stood impassively before Benjamin and

the girl, his expression unreadable. Although he was quite short, he made an impressive figure, Ben thought. He might be dressed in some sort of blue silk frock, but there was definitely no messing with him.

The man bowed low, his hands clasped together in front of him, palms together. "Honourable Sister," he said. His movements were slow and precise, in stark contrast to the hectic activity behind him. Ben had heard of these Chinese laundries before, but they were such a tight-knit lot he never thought that he would see inside one.

"Master Cho Jee," Ruby replied, matching his bow with one of her own.

He continued to eye Ben coldly though, leaving him in no doubt that his presence was not welcome.

"He's with me," she said, and that was apparently sufficient to appease Cho Jee, because he immediately gave another gracious bow and indicated a low table with a sweep of his hand.

"Please," he said crisply, "avail yourself of my humble hospitality." He bowed again as he retreated and left them alone. This time his robe parted slightly to reveal a meat cleaver strung to his belt. Ben had no doubt that the display was for his benefit and, as he settled himself cross-legged on a cushion, he wondered whether he had exchanged one set of troubles for another.

"Who's he?" Ben asked in a low whisper.

This time the girl with the emerald eyes did condescend to answer him. "A friend," she replied.

"And more to the point, who are you?"

"I'm a friend too," the girl replied. "That's all you need to know."

She might have had a gorgeous smile but her tongue was a little on the sharp side, Ben decided.

A moment later, Cho Jee appeared again, bringing them a pot of steaming hot chrysanthemum tea, before slipping back into the shadows. They sipped at it from tiny cups without handles, Ben keeping his thoughts to himself now.

He stirred his tea slowly with his left hand and, when he was sure that no one was looking, he slipped the spoon into his pocket. *Might be silver*, he thought.

As the silence stretched between them, Ben took in his surroundings. They were sat in a small corner of calm in an underground world of industry. Ben watched as Chinese men, women and children busied themselves at vast copper pots full of scalding hot water. Some scrubbed at dirty washing with waxy bars of carbolic soap, others worked it against washboards, their hands red from the boiling water. Men hauled the sheets from the cauldrons and then fed them through giant mangles, squeezing them dry. Then the clean sheets were strung from heavy lines across the ceiling, row upon row, like some huge armada setting out to sea.

Now that he had stopped running, Ben allowed himself to enjoy the softness of the cushion he sat on, the clean smell of the soap and the sweet comfort of the tea. He took a sideways glance at the girl and, in spite of the way that she spoke to him, he realized he was enjoying her company too.

"I'm Benjamin," he said with a grin. "Ben Kingdom."

"I know," the girl replied and, taking off her glove, she held out her hand. "Allow me to introduce myself," she said with a flourish. "I am Ruby Johnson."

He had no idea how she knew his name but he didn't think twice about taking her hand again. Her skin was warm and her grip was as firm as a man's. "Pleased to meet you, Ruby Johnson," he said.

"Likewise, Benjamin Kingdom," she replied.

It was Ruby who let go first. Ben took another sip of his tea. "So who were those roof-runners? Are you going to tell me now?"

"They were Watchers," said Ruby, no humour in her voice, her green eyes narrowing. She didn't elaborate further.

"And you're not a Watcher?"

"Definitely not," said Ruby. "I am...something else entirely."

Well, thank you, Miss Johnson, Ben thought sarcastically. *You are really making everything so much clearer.*

"So," she said abruptly. "Down to business."

"What?" said Ben.

"Business," said Ruby. "I find so much of life comes down to business, don't you? All you and I need do is settle on the amount for my reward and then let me bid you 'goodnight'."

"Your reward?"

"Of course," said Ruby. "You don't imagine that I go around rescuing people for free, do you?"

Ben hadn't been thinking along those lines at all. Suddenly it was not peaceful at all to be locked underground in a Chinese laundry with a girl that he didn't know and didn't understand, watched over by a mysterious man who gave every impression that his cleaver was not for show.

"What sort of reward did you have in mind?"

"Oh, nothing much," she said, almost casually. "A small silver coin should do it." She examined his face, looking for a reaction. "A Roman coin," she continued. "You do have one of those, don't you, Benjamin Kingdom?

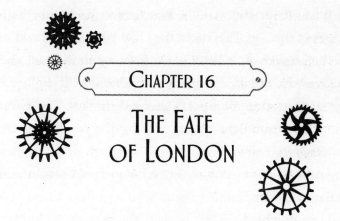

CHAPTER 16

THE FATE OF LONDON

"And you believe that Benjamin Kingdom is the one our prophets foresaw?" The old woman's voice cracked like lightning striking home. When she spoke, both angels and demons sat up and listened.

To her followers, she was Mother Shepherd. Her enemies called her by other, less flattering names: the Hag, the Witch Queen of Spies.

Jago Moon straightened his back and stood to attention as best as arthritis and the weight of years would allow. "I think that he *might* be," he said. "He definitely has the Touch, Great Mother. I've never felt it so strong before."

"Mmm," was all Mother Shepherd gave as a reply.

It was the tradition of the Watchers to meet in the high places of the city. That night they had been summoned to the bell tower of St Peter's, Dock Lane, an isolated and unloved church situated on the notorious Ratcliff Highway, breeding ground for the lawless and the lost. The wind whipped around the tower, making the candles gutter furiously in their sconce.

"And what about you, Lucy Lambert? What do you make of the boy?"

Lucy trembled slightly beneath the intensity of Mother Shepherd's gaze; her eyes, though old, were as clear and sharp as diamonds.

"Well, he seems..." *Nice*, she nearly said, and then brought herself up quick. *Benjamin Kingdom isn't "nice"*, she thought angrily, *he's a liability*. Lucy composed herself. "He seems reckless," she continued, "unreliable. A bit of an idiot."

"Mmm," said Mother Shepherd, then turned to the fourth member of their party; a man dressed all in black. "What are your thoughts, Brother?"

"His destiny is in his own hands," said the Weeping Man, his deep voice filling the belfry.

"But that's not good enough!" Lucy burst out, unable to hold the words back. "How can we trust him with the fate of the Watchers? With the fate of London?"

"It's the greatest mystery in the universe, isn't it?" said

Mother Shepherd. "I have never understood why our God would do something so foolish as to grant mere mortals free will; every single one of us containing the seeds of both our success and failure, each of us capable of great mercy or unspeakable evil." She allowed the full weight of her words to sink in. "Think of it…we face a thousand choices every day. A thousand opportunities to change the world for good or ill."

"But how can Ben be the one?" Lucy demanded. "The prophecy is so…"

"Vague?" Mother Shepherd suggested with surprising softness, and then she began to recite:

"One will come to lead the fight, to defeat the darkness,
bring the triumph of the light.
One will come with fire as his crown,
to bring the Legion tumbling down.
One will come with fire in his eyes,
to pierce through the veil of wicked lies.
One will come with fire in his heart,
to overcome all odds and play his part.
One will come with fire in his hand,
to purge the evil from this land."

The old woman smiled. "Faith is about trusting in what we cannot see."

"I know Ben Kingdom," said Jago Moon. "I know that

he's mouthy, and light-fingered, and cocky with it. But –" and here he lifted a gnarled finger – "were we any better when we were his age? I know I wasn't."

Mother Shepherd chuckled. "Well said, Mr. Moon."

Lucy wasn't convinced, but this time she managed to bite her tongue.

"What people don't see about Ben," Moon continued, "is the goodness in his heart and the struggles that he has overcome already."

"Well, seeing as how you already know so much about Benjamin Kingdom," said Mother Shepherd, "I suggest that you take him under your wing, Mr. Moon, and be quick about it."

"Yes, Great Mother," said Moon, although he hadn't the faintest idea of how he might win back the boy's confidence having scared him away so successfully.

"Benjamin might not seem worthy," said Mother Shepherd, "but he can change."

"He'll have to," Lucy muttered, not quite under her breath.

Slowly, Mother Shepherd turned and walked over to her side. She placed her gnarled hand on Lucy's shoulder and Lucy felt such tenderness, such safety, that she allowed the dam to burst within her and let her feelings come spilling out.

"I've fought for the Watchers my whole life," said Lucy, tears stinging her eye now. "You've been my mother, ever since…" The tears came more freely, and snot began to stream from her nose. Lucy cuffed it and continued. "I just can't bear the thought…"

"Shhh," said Mother Shepherd, smoothing the hair on the back of Lucy's head and letting the girl bury her face in her shoulder, snot and all. "I know," she went on, "and I've never doubted your love or your devotion to duty. But, in their own way, the years have taken their toll on both of us, haven't they?" She held the girl close. "My bones ache, Lucy. I'm tired of all this fighting. Don't you ever long for the war to be over?"

"With all my heart," Lucy replied without hesitation. "So long as I am on the winning side."

Mother Shepherd laughed. "Then you need to start having faith in Benjamin Kingdom," she said, "because if he is the Hand, then he *will* be the one to bring this war to an end."

Quietly, Lucy spoke the last lines of the prophecy:

"One will come to pay the cost; if he fails all is lost.

One will come in suffering and pain,
to know betrayal and be wounded again.

One will come to choose the way;
eternal darkness or the endless day."

Lucy paused. "Poor boy," she said. "But I have to ask what would happen if Ben chooses the Legion?" Her tears were replaced by a steely glare. "He's already more than halfway down that path. What if Ben becomes their leader instead of ours?"

"We have one great advantage," said Mother Shepherd. "The Legion only know that *we* are waiting for the arrival of the Hand of Heaven." She paused. "They don't know that the chosen one could equally turn out to be the Hand of Hell."

"But what if they corrupt him? Fill him with their lies?" Lucy asked again.

"*If* it is his destiny, then Benjamin Kingdom *will* become the Hand, nothing can stop that," said Mother Shepherd. "My most fervent prayer is that he joins the Watchers and fulfils his destiny as the Right Hand of Heaven." Her lips creased into a smile but there was no warmth in it. "However, if Ben turns his back on us and throws in his lot with the Legion, then he will rule them as the Left Hand of Hell."

"And then we'll be left to pick up the pieces, I suppose," said Moon.

"No, Mr. Moon, then we'll all be dead," she said flatly. "And I pity those left living."

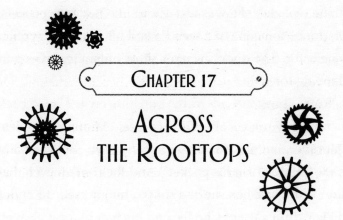

CHAPTER 17

ACROSS THE ROOFTOPS

In the end, they threw Ben out of the laundry. Literally.

Two of the Chinese men picked him up bodily, bundled him up the ladder and then tossed him out into the street. *I'm lucky to escape with me hat*, Ben thought, as he brushed himself down and tried to gather what remained of his dignity.

"Thanks for the tea!" he called with deliberate joviality, as the trapdoor was slammed and bolted against him. "Thanks for nothing, Ruby Johnson!"

The Coin, he thought angrily, as he stomped away. *This was all about the Coin.*

Ruby hadn't really been interested in helping him at

all, he realized; she was just out to line her own pockets. No doubt someone had seen Pa and his strange Egyptian benefactor. The docks weren't short on spying eyes and blabbing tongues.

Ruby Johnson had really put him on the spot back there. He'd tried to bluff, of course, claiming complete ignorance, but she wasn't having any of it. She'd actually made him turn out his pockets! And then, when even that didn't convince her, she had frisked him herself; all under the watchful gaze of Cho Jee and his handy meat cleaver. It had taken all of Ben's knack with sleight of hand to keep the Coin out of sight and even then it had been a close-run thing. She'd found the farthing but she'd let him keep that. He'd lost the silver spoon though, but since that wasn't really his, he probably shouldn't count it.

Still, thought Ben, *I didn't come away entirely empty-handed.*

When her search came up with nothing, Ruby had leaned towards him and placed a single, soft kiss on his forehead. "You'll just have to owe me," she'd breathed, before abandoning him, and disappearing behind the white sails of the sheets.

Ben didn't know how he felt about that kiss, and although it had made him feel warm at the time, it wasn't enough to keep out the savage cold now.

He buried his hands in his pockets and stamped off into the night.

He knew that he was running out of options. He couldn't go back to his room. He didn't dare find a quiet corner and doss down in case the Weeping Man came looking for him again. His father and brother were missing, Jago Moon was mixed up in this in ways he couldn't begin to think about, and Ruby Johnson had dropped him quicker than a hot coal. There was only one place left for him to go, and so he walked on through the night, sticking to the shadows, watching the rooftops, and trying, for once, to stay out of trouble.

He didn't spot anyone spying on him but that didn't mean that they weren't there. Who *were* the Watchers? Ruby hadn't given him any clues.

Ben thought about it all as he made his way along the embankment of the Thames. When he got to the De Keyser's Royal Hotel, he rummaged in the bins round the back and managed to find a stale roll before one of the kitchen hands saw him and chased him away with the promise of a whipping. The bread was hard and going green around the edges, but Ben chewed it industriously and it kept him going down Chancery Lane and High Holborn. It was the only thing to touch the inside of his belly since Mrs. McLennon's broth the morning before and his stomach growled in gratitude.

The sun was just scratching the sky when the British Museum finally came into sight: the grand expanse of the façade, two wings on either side; the great colonnade of Ionic columns, tall and proud; the statues in the portico standing guard, so real they could almost be alive. Professor Carter would be inside, he knew. He might even have some answers too.

In spite of the terrible fatigue that threatened to overwhelm him, Ben broke into a run, his aching feet breaking fresh snow until he fell down exhausted on the museum steps.

Even in that desperate state, without the energy left to lift his face up out of the snow, he found his hand irresistibly drawn to his pocket. Although he had only known trouble since it had arrived, his single clear thought before unconsciousness took him was this; keep the Coin hidden, keep it safe.

Instead of returning it to his trousers, he tucked it tight beneath the band of his hat, content that no one would think of looking there.

Sleep took him and held him tightly.

Ben did not see the Watcher with the scarred face, nestled quietly amongst the statues, patiently biding her time.

✳

Ben was woken by the smell of bacon and eggs. He wondered for a moment whether he had died in the snow and this was Heaven, and then he saw the face of Professor Carter looking down at him.

"Eat, boy," said the professor, his weather-beaten face a map of wrinkles as he smiled. "There's more where that came from."

Ben ate with the enthusiasm that only a starving boy can muster.

"I'm the same when I'm on expedition," said Carter. "When you don't know where your next meal is coming from, make the most of the one that you've got."

Ben looked from the professor's strong face to his great bone claw, and smiled. Could there be anyone better to come to your rescue? he wondered.

Carter settled back into the embrace of his leather chair, seeming to take great pleasure in watching Ben polish off a second rasher of greasy bacon and a thick slice of fresh bread.

In the comfort of Carter's room, surrounded by all the skulls and bones, the ancient objects from countries he had never heard of, Ben always felt absolutely safe and secure. Since that first day when he had brought the professor an arrowhead he had fished from the Thames,

Ben felt as if this should be his home.

Even as he thought that, he was filled with guilt for betraying his father. The last piece of bread was dry and difficult to swallow.

"So," said Carter, as the final mouthful went down, "why have you staggered halfway across London to die on my doorstep?"

Ben began his garbled story while Professor Carter sat and listened. Ben told him everything: about the Weeping Man and Jago Moon, about his room being destroyed, about Ruby and Mr. Smutts. The only thing he left out was the small fact that the Coin hadn't been stolen when his room was ransacked. It was right there in his hatband. Never out of his thoughts.

He wasn't even entirely sure why he was keeping the truth from the professor. It was peculiar, he thought, almost as if the Coin itself didn't want to be shared. When he had taken it from the hiding place in his room, his plan had been simple: to show the professor, get it valued and return it to his father. Now he had other ideas, and chief of those was to hang onto the Coin for a little while longer. It was his, wasn't it? Why should he share it with anyone?

When Ben was finished talking, Carter sucked the air between his teeth and his expression grew sombre.

"And now the Watchers have the Coin." Carter spoke quietly, his voice as dry as dust stirring in a crypt.

"I think they must have taken it when my room was destroyed," Ben lied.

Lucy Lambert stood on the edge and looked down.

Before this life, before the Watchers found her, the highest she had ever been was her father's shoulders. Now she was a denizen of the Above, the secret world of the Watchers. She could see the people walking along Whitechapel Road below, their hats pulled down firmly, their shoulders hunched up against the cold. None of them lifted their eyes towards her. She was as good as invisible on the roof of the London Hospital. She could have called out, but she knew her voice would never reach their ears.

Lucy became aware that she was not alone on the rooftop and turned to see a small girl, standing hand-in-hand with a powerful figure in a long black coat. It was the new girl, Molly Marbank, if she remembered rightly. Lucy smiled, her hand inadvertently rising to her face as she did so, covering the eyepatch and the scar: constant reminders of her own childhood. Molly made a sweet figure, Lucy thought. They had managed to find a Watcher long coat in something like her size; Molly looked as if she was playing dress-up in her father's clothes.

"It's time to go," said the Weeping Man, his deep voice both strong and tender at the same time. He was so full of contradictions, Lucy thought. The rumours were wrong, for one thing; he didn't cry all the time. Very often he would merely wear a serious expression on his face. Quite frequently he would even smile, and that was such a wonderful thing that the smile would almost take on a life of its own and run through the Watchers' camp, touching as many lips as it could.

He *did* cry, but only when something hurt him. And what normally hurt him, Lucy had discovered, was when other people felt pain. He cried for all the things that made Heaven sad. Some people called him the Weeping Man, but his real name was Josiah. Lucy only ever called him "sir".

She followed obediently and grinned as she saw the excitement on Molly's face. *How many years ago was that me?* Lucy asked herself.

"Follow me, little one," Josiah said to Molly.

Lucy brought up the rear while Molly meekly followed the Weeping Man back across the rooftop, studying where he put his feet and matching his every step across the tiles. Lucy could see Molly's six-year-old legs almost running in order to keep up with his purposeful strides. She knew that Molly was still learning, but speed was of the essence. It was a busy life being a Watcher, Lucy knew full well. There were plenty of cries for help in a city like London.

"Are you ready?" Josiah asked Molly as they neared the edge of the roof. Molly nodded vigorously. Lucy knew what was coming next; it was the most exhilarating and the most terrifying feeling in the world.

Josiah scooped Molly up and tucked her under one arm, as if she weighed no more than a bag of flour. Then the big man took half a dozen steps backwards across the flat roof of the London Hospital, adjusted his balance to account for the small girl he was carrying, and then ran, full pelt, towards the edge and the drop beyond.

Molly clung on with all her might, her tiny knuckles white, but Lucy knew that Josiah would never drop her. Or, at least, he hadn't dropped anyone before, as far as she knew. It was too late to say anything now though, because they were already in the air.

Lucy wished that she was on the ground at that moment, but only so that she could look up and see them making the jump from one rooftop to another. It was as if they were flying. Josiah's strong legs ran on nothing, his sure feet landing them safely on the other side. Lucy had lost count of the number of times she had seen Josiah jump, but the thrill had not diminished. If anything it was growing stronger.

Mostly the Watchers crossed the gap between buildings using extendable ladders, or death slides, or sometimes even pole vaults. But the most skilled boys had the gift, and Josiah was the most gifted of them all. Josiah made it look easy. He could leap and bound across rooftops and make seemingly impossible jumps with the grace of a mountain lion.

Sometimes Josiah reminded Lucy of her father. Not so much in the way that he looked – but in the way that he made you feel: safe. Protected. The boys said that the Watchers were an army, but really it was more like a big family, made up of children like her; the ones who had nothing in this world except each other. Boys and girls who tried to be brave, but were bruised inside or out.

Lucy watched as Molly and Josiah landed on the far side with a scrunch. And then she followed. With a small run-up, she threw herself into the arms of the air, trusting to experience that her momentum would carry her in an arc onto the lower roof on the other side of the road. The wind lifted her golden hair around her head and she could feel the smile splitting her face in two. It wasn't just the Watcher boys that could jump.

Lucy landed like a cat, her legs bent low, one hand

touching the roof tiles for balance. Then Molly reached for Josiah's hand and all three of them ran on across the rooftops together.

CHAPTER 18

LOOKING FOR TROUBLE

"I know the Watchers," Carter said. "Or more properly I should say I know *of* them. They are a…society, let's call them that, and my path and theirs have intersected a number of times in the past." He smiled grimly. "I know for a fact that they are established right across the Middle East," he continued. "I have had dealings with them in Jerusalem and Cairo with varying degrees of success." He said this with a sideways glance at the claw where his hand used to be. "I have reason to believe that there are smaller units operating right across the East." He began to list exotic names from his travels, while Ben sat enthralled. "In Carpathia; Transylvania; Constantinople, I'm certain of;

Moscow too probably, although I have no firm evidence of such. I even heard a rumour that there was a Watcher cell in Paris for a brief while, although I never did discover what they were doing there."

"But who are they?"

Carter took his time before replying, tapping the tip of his claw against his desk, not caring about the scars it left in the leather inlay.

"Who they are, I can't answer you," he said. "Their members change, their numbers rise and fall. One group can be scattered or disbanded, only for two more to spring up in their place. What I can tell you is this..." And he leaned forward as if to impart a great secret. "They take people, they brainwash them, they turn them into one of them and...I've devoted the best part of my life to working towards their destruction."

The boy looked surprised at that last remark.

"What?" said Carter. "You didn't think I spent all my time in this stuffy museum, did you?"

While they spoke, the professor observed the Kingdom boy intently, just as he would one of his specimens.

Ben was keeping something from him, obviously. The boy didn't have the Coin with him, he knew that much. He had gone through his pockets and searched inside his boots while Ben had been unconscious, but Carter was convinced that he wasn't being given the whole story. Did the Watchers really have it, as Ben suggested, or had the cunning lad stashed it somewhere? Carter smiled a thin smile. This is how it always starts when the Coins are at large; one lie leading to another, as the claws of evil begin to dig into your soul.

It occurred to Carter that nobody knew that Ben Kingdom was here. He looked at Ben and then at his own savage claw. There was nothing to stop him from making Ben tell him *everything*.

And yet he held back.

Whatever the truth was, the Watchers had already focused their attentions on Ben and so one way or another the boy's fate had become entangled with his own. He would keep Ben Kingdom close, Carter decided, if only to frustrate the Watchers' ambitions. There was definitely something about this boy which made him stand out from the other street rats, he thought.

"You should join me," Carter said, baiting his trap with flattery. "Men like you and I need to stand up against the Watchers."

He saw Ben's chest inflate and continued to pour on the honey. "You're clever, you're brave."

"Well..." said Ben, full of fake humility.

"Don't be modest, boy. How long have I known you?"

"Two years."

"No? I'd swear it was longer." Carter could see that Ben was lapping it up. "Anyway, I feel that I know you well enough to let you in on the biggest secret of my life. I'm not alone in my battle with the Watchers, Ben, I'm part of an army called the Legion and we are waging the oldest war the world has ever known."

One look at Ben's eyes convinced Carter that he had found a rich vein of curiosity and he continued to mine it deeply, talking at length about the glorious Legion and all that it could offer a young soldier like Ben. Careful to exclude any mention that it could cost him his life. And soul.

"Can you imagine it, Ben?" said Carter. "You and I, comrades in arms?" He came around the desk and put his hand on the boy's shoulder. "When a man is part of the Legion, he knows that his life stands for something; he can be proud of what he is doing. Do you know for certain that *your* life has purpose, Ben?"

"When I'm not learning how to make barrels, I fish other people's rubbish out of the stinking mud of the Thames," said Ben. "I'm getting by," he shrugged. "Purpose doesn't come into it."

"How would you like to travel the world with me, Ben? Break free from the petty rules that keep most of the human race penned up like sheep?" Carter's voice rose as he pushed home his advantage. "You could join me on my expeditions around the globe, help me to uncover new treasures, and when the call to arms comes we could fight side by side against Watcher oppression! Think about it, Ben, all that we could achieve together."

"But what about my father, my brother? I told you they were missing, remember?"

A flame of doubt showed on Ben's face, and Carter spoke quickly to stamp it out.

"Your family don't care for you, Benjamin. Haven't you worked that out yet? Your father is probably working an extra shift at the docks and never bothered to tell you. He'll be home again this evening and back to ignoring you as usual."

Carter realized too late that he had overplayed his hand. The flush of excitement left Ben's face, transforming it into a cold, granite slab.

"I'm going now, professor," said Ben.

"Wait!" said Carter. He grasped hold of Ben's coat, but not quickly enough to stop the boy from slipping out of it and sprinting towards the door. As a parting gesture, Ben slipped his fingers behind a tall glass display cabinet and, with surprising strength, sent it crashing towards the floor.

"Catch!" shouted Ben Kingdom, and then he was gone.

How dare Carter speak about his father like that?

Leaving the satisfying sound of breaking glass behind him, Ben stormed from the British Museum without once looking back. Outside the cold was waiting to bite at him, worse now that he had lost his coat too, but he welcomed it; the chill matched his mood. For a while he slouched along, kicking snow ahead of him. Then he heard the rapping of horse's hooves on the cobbles and, spotting a smart four-wheeler, decided that he would rather ride than walk.

He waited for the carriage to pass by and then quickly ran out into the road behind it. The trick here was twofold: to jump onto the footplate at the rear without being spotted by the driver, and then to keep your head down and not let go no matter what. Fortunately Ben was a past master. He leaped on, making it look easy, and was soon being carried down Drury Lane towards the Strand.

It wasn't long before he started to feel more like himself and he even started to cheekily doff his hat at some of the passers-by who spotted him taking his free ride on the back of the brougham. A woman with the starched collars and funereal expression of a governess appeared especially mortified by his audacity and he treated her to his most impudent grin.

"Well, really!" she exclaimed. Her expression was priceless and as Ben laughed out loud he felt some of his anger washing away.

He thought about Professor Carter's offer. Part of him *was* tempted. Who wouldn't want the opportunity to travel the world with a man of such learning? He imagined the sights that they might see together: pyramids in Egypt, lost tribes in Africa; all the things that he had read about and dreamed of late at night. And then there was the question of joining the Legion and he liked that idea too. Being part of a secret society, working in the shadows to keep London safe. Wouldn't that be the sort of life that any boy would yearn for?

Unfortunately, Ben couldn't forget what Carter had said about his family, and he wasn't sure that he could forgive him either. All this talk about treasure-hunting and ancient wars was all very well, but what about actually helping Ben to find his pa and Nathaniel?

When he considered Carter's callous words more calmly, Ben supposed that it *was* a possibility that Nathaniel and his father had stayed on at the docks for some reason and that nothing had happened to them... Yet the more he thought about it, the less likely it felt. Something inside told him that the Coin had brought trouble raining down on their heads too. They might have been hurt; they were certainly in danger. And it was up to him to sort it out.

He had hoped that Carter would help him track down his family, but he could forget about that now. There was no point in going to the police either. They'd never listen to a street urchin like him, especially if Constable Wilde had let slip the small incident of the manure-flavoured Christmas present that Ben had sent him. He was running out of ways to turn.

It seemed obvious that the Watchers had something to do with his father and brother disappearing, and that at least meant that he knew where to start his search. Mind made up, Ben hopped off the back of the carriage and waved at the driver, who, noticing Ben for the first time, returned Ben's wave with a clenched fist and a cheery line in blasphemy.

Happy to be taking matters into his own hands, Ben headed for home and ran through his three-step plan once more to test it for flaws. Firstly, he was going to borrow his brother's spare jacket. Secondly, he was going to climb up on the roof. And thirdly, he was going to go looking for trouble.

How can I fail?

CHAPTER 19

EVIL NEVER SLEEPS

"What do you mean, you gave our clothes away?" Ben needed to hear her say it again to make sure that he had got it right.

"I donated them to the Seaman's Mission," Mrs. McLennon explained. "It's a very worthy cause," she said.

"Since when were you allowed to dispose of possessions that don't belong to you?" Ben was outraged.

"You never said you'd be coming back," she stated, as if that made it suddenly alright.

Ben was too angry to speak. He flicked his gaze over Mrs. McLennon's shoulder, and when she turned to see who was behind her, he brushed past her and charged up the stairs, taking them two at a time. When he reached his room, it was as if he had gone into the wrong house by mistake.

All the broken furniture had been removed and the hole in the roof hastily patched with a sheet of tarpaulin. Mrs. McLennon had swept the room and hung a clean curtain at the window. There was a new washstand against the wall with a fresh china jug sitting on it. Where there had been three thin mattresses on the floor, now there was a single wooden bed, with a blanket stretched tight across it and a sailor's chest at its foot. And standing beside it was the sailor himself, who looked up with shock when he saw Ben.

"'Ere, what's your game?" the man bellowed through his seafaring beard.

Ben didn't have time to answer before Mrs. McLennon arrived on the landing behind him, panting heavily. Ben turned on her. "Why are you doing this? I live here!"

"That's where you are wrong, Benjamin Kingdom, and I would appreciate it if you didn't take that insolent tone with me."

The bushy-bearded sailor glowered, the veins standing proud on his neck. "Would you like me to put this young whippersnapper outside for you, Mrs. McLennon?" he asked. To Ben he looked like a bulldog, straining at the leash.

"I have had all of this behaviour that I can stand!" the widow declared. "Comings and goings in the night, disreputable people loitering around my door, such damage to my rooms – damage costs money, you know."

"What about my father and Nathaniel? How can they find me when they come back if you've put me out on the streets?" Ben protested.

"They won't be coming back," said Mrs. McLennon coldly. "A new ship was in, recruiting hands for a trip to the Americas. Doubtless that's where they have gone."

First Carter, now her, thought Ben. Was it so easy for everyone to believe that his own father and brother had just upped and left him?

A numbness took hold of Ben. His deepest fear was that his pa didn't want him. Was that what Mrs. McLennon saw when they sat together around the breakfast table?

She begun to usher him down the stairs towards the front door, the burly sailor backing her up, but Ben didn't have the strength to make a fight of it.

"Key," she said with outstretched hand as they stood on the threshold.

Mutely, Ben handed it over.

"I've destroyed those disgusting books you were reading too," she told him. "I put them all on the fire. No wonder you have no morals when you feed your mind with wild tales like that."

Ben wouldn't cry. He wouldn't give her that pleasure.

Mrs. McLennon paused then and pulled something from the pocket of her apron. "I'll not let you go out onto the streets empty-handed though," she said. "I do have a heart."

She put a small book in his hand and it was then that Ben really had to fight back the tears. He recognized it immediately; it was his mother's Bible. "I've repaired it as best I can," said Mrs. McLennon. "Keep it close now, you hear."

He would have thrown it back in her face there and then if it wasn't all that he had left to remind him of his family. Instead, he took it gratefully.

"We paid rent up until the end of the month," he said quietly.

"No refunds," she said firmly. And with that, yet another door was shut to him, never to be reopened.

Gazing out across the frozen Thames, Ben did a quick recount of his recent luck.

He was homeless, thanks to Mrs. McLennon's charity. He was unemployed, since Mr. Smutts's workshop had been burned to the ground, and he couldn't bed down there for the same reason. He had walked out on the professor and his pride wouldn't let him go back…not yet anyway. His father and Nathaniel were still missing; he refused to consider that they might have gone to sea and left him behind. He was being stalked by a group who called themselves the Watchers. Oh, and lest he forget, the Weeping Man who took children in the night was looking for him by name. What a great Christmas this was turning out to be.

Fat, wet flakes of snow fell on him and he reached into his pocket to touch the dog-eared Bible for comfort. For a second it was almost as if the soft, worn leather was his mother's hand…and then the moment was gone. In truth, Ben couldn't remember a happy Christmas.

In three days' time it would be 25th December. His birthday.

Christmas morning. When he was born and his mother died.

Merry Christmas, Ben.

Unlike Benjamin, Molly Marbank had food in her belly and a blanket across her shoulders. It was warm where she was, and dry, and although she missed her daddy every day, she was starting to feel safer and happier with the Watchers. Living so high above the ground was taking some getting used to, but she wasn't scared.

How could she be scared when the man who looked after her carried such a large sword?

Like all of the children in the Watchers, Molly had free rein of their camp, although she did have to stay out of the way sometimes when the grown-ups were setting up. The Watchers never slept in the same place twice, which meant that every morning there was a great deal of work to do: packing up their equipment, cooking pots, sleeping mats, oil lamps, ladders and crossing planks; taking down the canvas shelters that they erected each night, stowing the poles, coiling the ropes. Mother Shepherd always chose where they would stay. She would go and pray quietly and then come and tell everyone where the Uncreated One had guided her to.

Since she had been rescued, Molly had slept soundly beneath canvas on the roof of the Bank of England, the roof of the French Embassy – with a lovely view over Hyde Park – and had spent last night on the roof of the Elephant and Castle Theatre, New Kent Road, listening to the music rising up through the rafters. Before that she had been sleeping in the gutter and in doorways, so she really felt that she was going up in the world.

Tonight Mother Shepherd said that they would be camping on the roof of Liverpool Street Station, so once again everyone was hard at work breaking down the tents and getting ready for a long trek. There wasn't very much that Molly could do and, spotting Josiah sitting quietly, she skipped over to join him. She was always full of questions and her new best friend always had an answer.

He was running a whetstone along the edge of his sword to keep it sharp. When he spotted her, he looked up with a smile.

"Hello, little one," he said.

Molly beamed and moved closer so that she was standing next to him. Josiah's sword was beautiful she thought, if swords could be beautiful. It shone like silver, even on a cloudy day.

"What does that say?" she asked, pointing to a word engraved on its blade.

"It says *Peace*," Josiah replied. "That's what my sword is called."

Molly nodded. "Do all swords have names?"

"They do in my family," he said softly.

Taking an oiled cloth, he smoothed it over the length of the blade and then slid *Peace* back into her sheath. Molly could see that Josiah was looking unhappy again. She reached out with her fingers and touched the dark locks of his hair that tumbled around his face.

"Why are you sad, Josiah?"

"Because I think I'm going to have to use my sword for the first time," he said.

"Why?"

"Because evil never sleeps," Josiah replied.

A single tear rolled from his eye and Molly used her fingers to brush it away.

"You'll be alright, Josiah," said Molly.

Josiah didn't answer.

How dare he?

Claw Carter sifted through the debris of his display cabinet, taking out the bigger shards of broken bone in the hope that some of his treasures might yet be rescued. He picked up half a human jaw, then dropped it again in despair. It had taken him nine months to travel up the Amazon to steal the sacred skull of the Bat People; it hardly seemed worth the effort now. Rising to his feet, he paused for an instant and then ground it into dust with his heel, stamping out his fury. He was not accustomed to being turned down, and certainly not by a mere boy.

Still, Ben Kingdom knew how to make an exit, he'd give him that.

There was definitely more to the lad than met the eye. He could see why the Watchers would be so keen to make him one of theirs; Ben wasn't your common-or-garden street rat.

One of the privileges that came with being a knight commander of the Legion was that Carter had access to the Dark Library, hidden deep within the Under. There was no other library of its kind in the world. What wonders it held! What treasures! Scrolls that had been rescued from the blaze of Mesopotamia; lost volumes of ancient knowledge; every book that the Holy Roman church had declared blasphemous; everything that was forbidden...they were all there.

Professor Claw Carter read the same way that he ate: voraciously. He had gorged himself in the Dark Library, ripping out the blood-red secrets until he was full. It was a historian's dream, to possess all the secrets of the ancient world, and he didn't stop to count the hours that he had spent pursuing that goal. More importantly, it gave Carter the upper hand. The Council of Seven never deigned to enter the Library; perhaps they considered themselves above something as menial as learning, Carter mused. Whatever the reason for their complacency, it left room for a man of ambition like him. Wars were won by the man who knew his enemy's weaknesses and who had learned from the lessons of the past. Knowledge was power.

Within the cold calculating machine of Professor Carter's mind a cog turned, and thoughts of Ben Kingdom clicked into place with a fragment of forbidden text.

The conclusion was so sudden, so shocking, that Claw Carter stopped in his tracks.

A ranting madman had written of a boy. A boy who had the potential to channel the power of Heaven or Hell. A boy born on the Saviour's Day, who could overthrow the rule of law and usher in the days of chaos; if he so chose.

A boy with red hair.

Carter was dragging on his coat even as he left his rooms. He had been wrong the first time. He'd thought that flattery was the bait to snare Ben Kingdom, but the boy had wriggled off that hook. It was time to try a different sort of lure.

Ben had been watching the baked potato man for about five minutes, planning his move. It would have been easier to buy one, but all he had in his pockets was a farthing and that wouldn't stretch. He had the silver Coin too, but that wasn't for wasting on luxuries like food. So while he savoured the taste of butter and pepper on the air, and tried to ignore the salt and stink of the Thames, Ben waited for his chance.

The vendor was an old sailor, with grizzled whiskers and a wooden leg. Ben could see that the man was standing so close to his brazier full of burning coals that his false leg was beginning to smoke slightly. If it caught on fire that would be a good diversion, he thought, although he probably didn't want to hang around that long.

There was a fair crowd around the potato seller and Ben edged his way in, being careful not to make any sudden moves or do anything that might catch the man's eye. *Softly softly, catchy monkey*, Ben thought to himself, drawing his hand up inside his sleeve so that he wouldn't burn his fingers when he went for the grab. *Just a little closer…*

He was inches away when a hand clasped his wrist fast and a voice whispered sharply in his ear. "Hold it right there, sunshine."

That's it, Ben thought, *the game's up.*

Then he took a closer look at the hand. The green-gloved hand.

"That was the most amateur approach at a swipe I've seen in a long time," the girl said.

"Ruby Johnson!" exclaimed Ben, surprised at how pleased he was to see her, considering that she'd left him in the lurch last time.

"The very same," she said, her eyes all wide and innocent. "I'm like a bad penny, aren't I? I just keep turning up."

CHAPTER 20

INTO THE UNDER

In all his life, Ben had never met a girl quite like Ruby Johnson.

She was wearing velvet trousers for one thing, which was quite shocking for a girl, even if she undeniably suited them. She was different to the girls on Old Gravel Lane, who were mainly rough as rats, in Ben's opinion. No, Ruby had class. She was different to the girls in Mr. Cowper's ragged school too. They were quiet and serious, speaking only when spoken to and scribbling studiously on their slates rather than meeting his eye. Ruby Johnson's eyes, by contrast, were almost inescapable. They were always on him, sometimes with such blazing intensity that he didn't know how to cope and had to snatch his gaze away before he got burned.

Ruby's eyes were simply dazzling, Ben thought; the sort of jewels that men might fight for.

For the remainder of the day, Ruby led Ben through the city and he looked on with a smile as she cast her spell everywhere they went. At the Jackdaw Inn, one flash of those emerald eyes gained them the best seats in the house and a steak and ale pie apiece, all courtesy of the florid landlord and absolutely gratis. In a quiet corner of Soho, a German Jewish tailor provided Ben with the first new jacket he had ever owned, and instead of taking money, the man had kissed Ruby's gloved hand and thanked *her* for coming.

"I can't have you dressed as a ragamuffin if you're going to be seen with me," she said with a laugh. Ben laughed too, and without him really noticing, the hours slipped by. Somehow, when he was with Ruby, all his troubles seemed far away.

A church bell chiming ten reminded Ben how late the hour, how cold the night, and how very homeless he was. "Ruby," he said, "I'm grateful for everything that you've done for me so far…"

"It's nothing," she said, her teeth glinting white in the moon's glow.

"...but I was wondering what the plan was. Have you got a billet somewhere where we can get our heads down or should we make our way to the river, try to find some shelter under a bridge?"

Ruby tossed back her head and laughed. It was a beautiful sound but it still managed to annoy him. He wasn't some child to be led around by the hand for her amusement.

"If you're going to make fun of me then—"

She silenced him with one touch of her gloved finger to his lips. "Hush now, Benjamin Kingdom, I'm laughing because the night has only just begun."

And with that, she padded away down the lane. In the near distance, a drunken fight had broken out and the sounds of violence were getting closer.

"Well, are you coming or not?" said Ruby.

Ben stood his ground, hands shoved deep into his pockets. "Not until you tell me where we're going."

"You're not afraid of ghosts, are you, Ben?" she asked with a smile.

The gate was locked and chained. On the other side of the wall, weeds and brambles had run riot, and as Ben looked through the bars, he could see statues of lonely angels, still crying silently over loved ones lost. *All in all, I would much rather sleep under a bridge*, he thought.

"Give me a bunk-up then," said Ruby cheerfully. Ben made a stirrup of his hands and hoisted Ruby onto the top of the crumbling wall. Then he scrambled up after her. She had taken him to a cemetery just off the Tottenham Court Road.

"Whitefield's burial ground," said Ruby, still grinning. "Over twenty thousand bodies were buried here before they discovered that it wasn't consecrated ground. It was quite a scandal at the time," she added, hopping down among the graves.

If it weren't for her smile, Ben would have left her there and then. As it was, he lowered himself down off the wall and followed her through the garden of the dead. The snow was crisp and unbroken, a heavy blanket for all those sleeping beneath the soil. Ben trod carefully.

"What are we doing here?" he asked, annoyance telling in his voice.

Ruby didn't answer, but instead brought him to a crumbling vault. Ben looked at the knotted ivy around the door, and the carved skull smiling back at him with a rictus grin. Ruby discovered another carving beneath the twisted vines, a gauntlet clenched into a fist. For reasons that she wasn't sharing with Ben, it made her smile.

Satisfied that she had found what she was looking for, Ruby put her shoulder to the door and it gave an inch. "In we go," she said lightly.

"You have got to be kidding," said Ben. "I can find us somewhere much better than this." *Almost anywhere*, he added privately.

"Trust me," she said and pushed the door open wide enough to slip inside.

Ben followed with a sigh. It was even colder inside the tomb than it was in the graveyard. "This is stupid," he said.

Enough moonlight braved the gloom to catch Ruby's green eyes. "Just trust me," she repeated, and then, getting down on her knees, she began to smooth her hands over the flagstones. Her searching fingers quickly uncovered a heavy circle of metal, which she grabbed with both hands.

"When I say 'lift' we both lift, understand?" she said.

Those emeralds gleamed in the starlight.

"Lift!"

Ben lifted.

From beneath the flagstone, a wave of hot air rose to meet them, bringing with it the warm glow of candlelight. Ben looked over the edge and saw a carved flight of steps leading down.

"Where are we going?" said Ben.

"Into the Under," said Ruby, with a smile.

Day Four
23rd December, 1891

CHAPTER 21

THE LOST

There were so many questions in Ben's head all shouting for his attention.

Ruby paused only to drag the flagstone back into place behind them, before leading him down the spiral staircase. He followed her down the steps and into an arched tunnel that stretched away in both directions. The vaulted roof was high enough for him to walk without having to stoop, although he could easily touch it if he reached up. There were cobwebs in the corners, but one glance at the foot-worn floor was enough to tell him that this passageway was far from abandoned. The other big clue was the candles, which burned in sconces the length of the tunnel, creating just enough light to give strength to the shadows.

"How did you know how to find this place?"

She smiled. "It found me."

Ben's jaw clenched involuntarily. For someone so beautiful, she really could be very annoying. "How did you know about the trapdoor?" he tried again.

"You know how to get into your own house, don't you?" she answered glibly.

Ben gritted his teeth. Did she do it on purpose? he wondered. "Where are you taking me?"

"You'll see," she said over her shoulder, although this time without the usual jaunty bounce in her step.

Ben had little choice but to follow her deeper into the strange warren. Although he liked Ruby, he realized that he didn't know very much about her. She was fun, certainly, but she was also a dangerous, unpredictable creature; he had best be on his guard.

As they made their way deeper into the maze of tunnels, they passed arched doorways and openings, although there was no clue as to where they might lead. Sometimes Ben could make out voices, echoing and hollow, but the words escaped him and only served to add to his sense of disorientation. In the London he knew, the one above his head, Ben considered himself to be king of the streets. Here in the Under he was lost, and every step took him further from the surface and safety.

"So how do you find your way down here?" Ben asked after a while. He sensed her warming to him again and wanted to test the waters.

"Look up," Ruby said, pointing to the vaulted ceiling. Ben followed her gaze and saw some writing in an alphabet he had never seen before. "That marking tells me that we are directly underneath Goodge Street."

Ruby took his hand again and bounced up to the next junction. "That way to the basement of Madame Tussaud's, sir, and that way to the dungeons of the Bloody Tower," she said in her best cockney accent.

The enormity of this labyrinth was beginning to set in and Ben let out a low whistle. "Who made all these tunnels? It must have taken years."

"You don't know the half of it," said Ruby. "The work started over three hundred years ago and it's not finished yet." She paused. "Have you heard of Sir Alasdair Valentine?" She saw his blank expression. "I'm not surprised, few people on the surface have."

"Who's he?"

"That depends on who you ask." She shrugged. "Some people see him as a traitor, others as a hero. It all comes down to which side you're on, I suppose." She looked full into Ben's eyes then, as if challenging him to say something.

Ben wished that he had a sister; it might have given him some small chance to understand the way that Ruby thought. He chose to ignore the look and say nothing. It seemed to do the trick.

Ruby continued. "Valentine was Spymaster General for King Henry VIII and an ordained priest...amongst other things." Ben didn't understand the implications of that comment either, but held his tongue. "When the old King was at the height of his madness," Ruby explained, "riddled with disease, desperate for a wife who would give him a son, estranged from the Pope and at loggerheads with most of Europe, he became increasingly paranoid; suspicious of anyone and everyone. It was Valentine who came up with the idea of digging a network of tunnels, so that Henry could travel in secret or escape in the middle of the night if the need arose. Unfortunately for Valentine, he clashed with the King one too many times and ended up with his head on a spike for a 'thank you' and the promise of death for anyone who ever dared to mention his name," Ruby said with some resentment. "But that was the start of the Under."

"And the work has never stopped?" Ben was amazed.

Ruby answered with pride. "We can travel to almost

any destination in London," she said, "without once having to put our heads above the surface."

"And who is 'we'?" Ben asked. "Who lives down here, out of the light?"

"People like you and me, Benjamin. Unwanted kids. All the ones that society doesn't know what to do with. The throwaways and the runaways. The abandoned. The broken. The lost. Some of us are hiding, some of us are trying to escape. Most of us are just trying to live."

"The Legion," said Benjamin.

"Yes, the Legion," Ruby replied. "For we are many."

It occurred to Ruby that she had already said too much.

It was important to remember why she had brought Kingdom here and it had nothing to do with charity. She wished that Ben could be more disagreeable or repellent in some way. As it was, she was starting to like him, and that would never do. She was part of the Legion, she reminded herself, she had made certain promises; emotion didn't come into it.

Ben looked at her, all puppy-dog eyes, waiting for her to throw another morsel for him to catch. Well, he would have to go hungry.

He was asking more questions and jumping along at

her side and she ignored him steadfastly, fixing her eyes straight ahead.

"Nearly there now," she said coldly.

Ben really didn't understand Ruby.

One minute she was his best friend, all toothy grins and big eyes, the next she was treating him like a bad smell: pretending he wasn't there and wishing he would go away. *Are all girls like this?* he wondered.

Ben felt like that stupid pudding-faced innkeeper who gave away his pies in return for one of Ruby's smiles. Was he just another monkey who danced for her delight whenever she clapped her hands?

It really was a shame that she had such a wonderful smile.

He continued by her side through the warren of tunnels and side tunnels. She had stopped answering his questions and he had stopped asking them. Instead he was trying to gain his bearings, although without the familiar landmarks and the London skyline to guide him, it wasn't easy. Ruby obviously knew these subterranean streets as well as he knew Shoreditch, but for the minute he couldn't even tell east from west, and until he learned how to read the orientation markers on the ceiling, there was no way that he could make it out of this rats' nest on his own.

And rats' nest it was, regardless of Ruby's assurances that the dwellers of the Under were just like him.

The top corridors had been deserted, but as they went further into the heart of the maze, it was becoming as crowded as Mrs. McLennon's had been. Body packed beside body, fighting for space and air. The atmosphere reminded him of Mrs. McLennon's too: there were children crying, husbands and wives shouting, men with too much drink in them challenging the world. As much as he hated Ruby Johnson at that moment, he was glad that he wasn't here alone.

A dark-eyed man in a battered Navy uniform approached from the other end of the corridor. He made as if to let them pass and then deliberately clipped Ben with his shoulder, spinning him around. Ben said nothing and fixed his own gaze ahead and centre. *Keep your head down*, he told himself.

As they walked, he tried to understand the sort of society that had been created here, away from the eyes of the sun. As far as he could make out, although there were definitely locked doors which hid secrets of their own and some areas that appeared to be reserved for the higher levels of this community, most of the living quarters themselves were communal. They took the form of caverns carved from the living rock, with arched ceilings and fire pits for cooking and warmth. There were chairs and other pieces of furniture that had been manhandled down from the surface, even some scraps of carpet here and there, mismatched and ragged, like the inhabitants.

Coffin-sized niches had been cut into the walls, hung with makeshift curtains to allow the dwellers some degree of modesty. He had expected the air to be rank with so many people living on top of one another, but though there was a rich haze of coal smoke, tobacco, cooking smells and the musk of hot bodies, it was not totally unpleasant and certainly no worse than Old Gravel Lane on a summer's day.

All around him, Ben saw the denizens of the Under stretching, yawning, scratching, talking, taking their supper, sipping hot tea, laughing, smoking a pipe before settling down for bed; all just as they might have done in the world above.

As he began to feel more confident, Ben let his eyes wander further. He noticed small circular openings in the ceilings, which he surmised must ultimately find their way to the surface as chimneys, venting away the combined smoke of fires, candles, torches and lanterns. There were also wells full of fresh clean water, which came bubbling up from deep within the London loam, and, here and there, impressive mechanical devices which resembled huge leather bellows. They were powered by waterwheels constantly turning in man-made watercourses, and he guessed these were the lungs of the Under, drawing down clean air and saving them all from suffocation.

Just then, the ground beneath Ben's feet began to shudder, and he was filled with a sudden vision of caving roofs and crushed bodies, including, most alarmingly, his own. It started with a vibration in the flagstones, and then grew until it filled the length of the passageway with a deafening roar; part animal, part machine. Ben's own legs shook and he brought his arms up to cover his head. Thundering, rattling, hissing, the wave of sound engulfed him and he braced himself for the worst.

Nothing happened.

The noise diminished, the tremors ceased, and the danger merely slipped away. And the strangest thing about it, Ben thought, was that no one else had paid it a blind bit of notice.

At his side, Ruby Johnson was trying, and failing, to disguise her smile. Ben brought his arms down, feeling somewhat self-conscious, and tried to make it look as if he'd simply been having a stretch. Ruby Johnson sniggered. *The Underground!* Ben twigged a second later.

"It was a train, wasn't it?" he asked quietly.

Ruby nodded.

"Did I look very stupid?"

Ruby nodded again.

In truth, Ben didn't know how he felt about the Under. All these tunnels, all these secrets. The size and scope of this hidden world, the ingenuity which created and maintained it, the fact that it even existed, were all incredible. He also liked the idea that you could get a second chance. London was a harsh place and he had known lots of good people fall down through no fault of their own and never gain their feet again.

Lost your job? Bad luck. Got sick? Bad luck. Can't pay the rent? Feed the kids? Clothe your wife? So sorry, old boy, bad luck. It pleased Ben to imagine that there was a safety net below the city, waiting to catch those who fell.

Yet for all those positives, there was something about the Under that put him on guard. There was a hot taste of menace in the air. Like embers blown over a field of dry wheat; it would take nothing for the whole place to go up. Yes, they were free from the harsh injustices of the law down here, but they were also free from the law's protection.

Ben saw the homeless – dry, safe, and out of the cold – and he was pleased for them. Babes snuggled in their mothers' arms, families facing a new future together, holding tight after the storm. But, he also saw faces full of anger and resentment, bitter with the world for reducing them to this. Army deserters stood side by side with disgraced noblemen, swindlers, cheats and thieves. There were faces here that he recognized from the docks, faces of fighters and drinkers. He saw the face of a murderer, a perfect likeness of his *Wanted* poster. Hard faces with angry eyes. And not one of them repentant.

No law, so no one to judge them.

No law here but that which they made for themselves.

Finally Ruby brought him to a door, and almost roughly pushed him towards it.

"Where am I?" asked Ben.

"You'll see," she said curtly. "Wait here." Then she turned on her heel and walked away.

Thank you, Ruby, Ben thought angrily. *Thank you very much.*

CHAPTER 22

THE OTHER SIDE OF THE DOOR

It was a strong door. Solid, and somehow intimidating. But Benjamin was not afraid. He was bristling with anger. And he was quite enjoying it. It was the clearest emotion he had felt in a long time.

Ruby had left him, and he could either stand there like a lemon waiting for her, or he could take matters into his own hands. Without hesitation he took the handle and began to turn it. He wanted to see what was on the other side of the door.

He opened it slowly, to be on the safe side, and was rather disappointed by what he found. At first glance, this room didn't appear to be that different from any other he had seen in the Under. There was a stout table with playing cards scattered across it, the remains of a roast chicken, a number of battered chairs, a few personal belongings and not much else. He stepped inside; he could at least sit down until Ruby deigned to return for him.

At the far end of the room was a fireplace, but the fire had died down and so the only light came from a metal sconce on the low ceiling, the candles flickering wildly. He dragged a chair over to the fire and began to rake at the embers with a poker.

It was only then that he thought twice about the thick, dark curtains that hung the length of both walls. Ben looked at them with a growing sense of dread. One of the curtains twitched and he knew that it could only mean one thing.

He was not alone.

All around him the filthy fabric was being drawn aside to reveal the dwellers of the Under, stacked on top of each other like bodies in a tomb. Bodies that were stirring, rising from their sleep.

Something deep inside Ben warned him that he could be in for a rough ride here and so he rolled up his sleeves and braced himself. He had no idea how many opponents he might have to deal with, but he vowed to live long enough to tell Ruby Johnson exactly what he thought of her for getting him into this mess.

One by one the figures swung their legs over the edge of their bunks. Ben counted them in the dim light; two on his left, three on his right. The odds could have been much worse, but unless they were going to challenge him to a game of whist, he knew that he was probably in for a bit of a pasting.

As his eyes became accustomed to the gloom, he saw to his relief that he was facing the sort of boys that he bumped up against all the time on Old Gravel Lane. He had been half expecting to find himself up against ex-soldiers discharged from Her Majesty's service for conduct unbecoming. However, all the lads were hanging back for some reason, and Ben got the feeling that they were waiting for the last member of their group, still hidden behind the remaining curtain.

The figure that finally emerged was tall and angular; all bones and sharp corners. Like the other residents of the room, he wasn't much older than Ben, although his lanky height gave him added years. His hair was a sharp white-blond and hung in loose natural curls that were almost feminine. His eyes, even in the candlelight, were the fiercest blue. He looked like an angel.

No, Ben corrected himself as those blue eyes locked on

him with disdain; he looked like a fallen angel, full to overflowing with resentment and pride.

"So what have we here, then?" said the young man in an educated voice, which instantly set Ben's hackles rising.

"An intruder, Captain," said one of the boys.

Captain? thought Ben. *How la-di-da.* "No, a guest," he said out loud. "Ruby Johnson brought me."

"Well," declared the captain, "since our very own Miss Ruby invited you here…" The whole room waited on his pronouncement. "…it would be terribly rude for us not to make our guest feel at home.

"First, some introductions." He swept his long bony arm around the room in an extravagant display of welcome. "This gentleman is my personal squire, Jimmy Dips, and these other fine fellows are John Bedlam, Hans Schulman and the esteemed Alexander Valentine, all knights of the Legion." At this point, a hunchbacked boy struggled up from his bunk and shuffled towards the remains of the fire, a crippled bulldog hopping along beside him. "Not forgetting our unfortunate friend," the captain continued. "This is squire Munro, and his three-legged companion is Buster.

"And I," he said, with a long-fingered hand splayed decorously on his own chest, "am the Honourable Lord

Rupert Mickelwhite, Captain of the Legion and third Duke of Gloucester. You may call me 'My Lord', or possibly 'sir' if you get to know me better."

"Take no notice of his nibs," said John Bedlam, a small lad, shorter than Ben but with a stocky build and a cocky manner. He sauntered over and took Ben's hand, squeezing it firmly, almost too hard, as if testing to see whether Ben would wince. Ben didn't. Bedlam returned to his bunk.

"We are pleased to make your acquaintance." It was Schulman's turn to speak and his accent betrayed his German heritage. Schulman struck an imposing figure, tall and broad, with the build of a blacksmith and long fair hair that hung around his face like a mane. Schulman slapped Ben heartily on the back with enough force to make him take an involuntary step forwards. The German laughed then, but it was not an unfriendly sound.

Munro and Buster had repositioned themselves so as to make the best of the dying embers in the grate. One of them broke wind thunderously, although Ben wasn't sure whether it was the crookback or his dog. Jimmy Dips, meanwhile, had moved across the barracks to stand obediently at Captain Mickelwhite's side. Jimmy had a twitchy rat-like face and a slightly oily manner, almost too eager to please.

"Forgive me if I don't get up," said Alexander Valentine,

still sprawled on his bunk. The boy had a pale, thin face, with tight lips and cheekbones that stood out harshly beneath stretched skin. The hand that emerged from beneath the blanket to give a regal wave was almost skeletal. Was this some distant relation of the mysterious Alasdair Valentine? Ben wondered.

On the whole, Ben didn't consider them to be a bad group of lads. He gave one and all the benefit of his broadest grin, tipped a finger to his hat as a salute and to take a sneaky check to make sure that the Coin was still safe and sound, and then extended the hand of friendship towards Mickelwhite. He was a toffee-nosed git, Ben thought, but he might be alright underneath.

"The name's Benjamin Kingdom," he said, still grinning.

Mickelwhite took Ben's hand in a cold clammy grasp and then, without warning, twisted round and wrenched Ben's hand up vigorously behind his back. Ben bent double in pain.

"You forgot to say 'My Lord'," Mickelwhite hissed in Ben's ear.

Ben knew that gangs had their initiation ceremonies and so he took the assault as a good sign, although he wasn't enjoying having his arm twisted so far up his back that he could easily believe it might snap. The Old Gravel Lane boys had a similar ritual, which involved a fair amount of fighting and then the most sacred part of the investiture: the ceremonial stealing of a pork pie. Ben was waiting for the pain to start easing up and the laughter to begin. His eyes began to water. *Any time now, lads.*

Mickelwhite brought his face level with Ben's. "Come on, boy," he hissed. "You're in the presence of your superiors: *on your knees.*"

This was clearly part of the test and, determined not to be found wanting, Ben resisted with all his strength. "Never," he replied.

Someone behind him – John Bedlam, Ben guessed – kicked him in the crook of his legs, which buckled painfully beneath him.

"Ease up," said Ben, as light-heartedly as he could manage. "Let's just be mates."

"Let's just be mates, *My Lord.*"

A knee found his belly and left him gasping. *Clearly some gangs have stricter rules than others,* he thought, but he kept his lips firmly buttoned. A fist hammered into the small of his back. A booted foot dragged down his shins.

"So this is the famous Ben Kingdom," said Mickelwhite mockingly. "I was expecting someone far more impressive than you!"

Of course Ben could have stopped them easily by simply grovelling like Mickelwhite wanted him to. The problem was that Ben wasn't about to start bowing and scraping to anyone.

An arm clenched around his throat and began to squeeze. Ben's ears filled with the sound of his own blood roaring. That made Ben smile even as his face turned blue. Mickelwhite wasn't as clever as he thought he was; Ben wouldn't be able to call anybody "My Lord" with a crushed windpipe, would he? It was only a small consolation however, because he would be unconscious in a couple of seconds. Or possibly dead.

All at once, Mickelwhite released him and all the boys stepped backwards, leaving Ben gasping on the floor.

I've won! Ben told himself triumphantly as he massaged his bruised throat.

Then he saw why they had stopped.

Then again, thought Ben, *maybe not.*

Chapter 23

From Saint to Sinner

Benjamin Kingdom is not best pleased to see me. That was Carter's first thought, as he stood in the doorway with Ruby Johnson at his side. When they saw him, the young men in Captain Mickelwhite's brigade slapped their clenched left fists to their right shoulders in the Legion salute, which Carter returned, but his gaze never left Ben.

There was such a lot of anger in that young man. Carter could see it in his eyes and the defiance of his stance. He smiled; that would be a very useful attribute if it could be channelled in the right direction. He remembered the secret writings in the Dark Library; rage had always been a favourite tool of the Legion, and Ben Kingdom was full to the brim. One little push might be all it took for Ben to start irrevocably down the black path that would lead to his destiny as the Hand of Hell. And Carter's own personal champion, naturally.

The Watchers were very keen on mercy and forgiveness, which some would say was to their credit, but in the matter of war, Carter always found wrath to be a far more effective weapon.

"Benjamin," he said, performing a pantomime of concern. "Thank goodness you're safe! I'm relieved that Miss Johnson was able to find you. I have some bad news for you, Ben."

"I'm listening." Ben was still incensed, but Carter could see that he had piqued his interest. Carter spun the moment out a little longer, keeping Ben in anticipation.

"It's your brother Nathaniel, I'm afraid," he said sombrely. "The Watchers have captured him."

"What? How? And what do you care anyway?" Ben spat back at him. "When I came to you, you didn't want to lift a finger for my family."

"I was wrong, Ben," said Carter, continuing to pour out soothing words. "I was so excited about the prospect of you joining me in the Legion that I lost sight of what was really important."

"So you'll help me rescue Nathaniel? Find my pa?" The

tone of Ben's voice had changed and Carter knew that he was winning.

"I'll do everything I can," said Carter, and the look of relief on Ben's face told him that the battle was his.

"I'm so glad that we are seeing eye to eye again, Ben." Carter smiled, and for a fraction of a second Ben smiled back. If Ben *was* going to be the Hand, it was important for the Legion to stake their claim before the Watchers had their chance. He pushed his advantage home. "We *will* rescue Nathaniel," Carter continued, "but first I want you to do something for me."

"Name it," said Ben. "And then we can get going."

It was all too easy, Carter thought.

"Captain Mickelwhite, please be so kind as to stoke up the fire."

"I'm sorry to disturb you, Great Mother, but I bring news."

Mother Shepherd knew from the tone of Jago Moon's voice that the matter was grave. She moved slowly, using the time to prepare herself. Age had made a slave of her limbs but that didn't matter to her; she didn't have to hurry for anyone. In all her long years, she had learned a thing or two, and if she had any virtues, then patience was one of them. How much of her life had been spent rushing, imagining that speed was of the essence? She knew that it was possible to race your whole life away and never stop for a moment and pause to consider those things that truly mattered.

Issues of life.

And death.

And what comes after.

She supposed that the church they were in must be cold; these huge echoing buildings always were. Yet she did not feel a chill in her old bones. Candlelight warmed a path ahead of her, but the real fire was the one that stirred her heart. The spark of her God, the Uncreated One, inside her soul. She could feel it; a living, breathing, palpable presence. It gave direction to her life and purpose to her steps.

She was content that the eyrie was well placed for the night, safely established on top of the Old Bailey. Everyone had shared in mutton broth and bread, and the young ones were bedded down and sleeping, so she had taken the opportunity to slip away and pray, just as she had done for the last seventy-something years.

The Watchers were not part of any church; they did not have the Papal seal of approval or the blessing of the Anglican synod. However, there were many good church men and women across the denominations that supported them in secret. Some gave food for the orphans they cared for; others prayed for them; others still opened their doors in the dead of night, allowing Mother Shepherd and her flock to find refuge until morning.

It scared her to think that it all might change. If the Legion had their way, she and all her children would be hunted down like dogs.

And if Benjamin Kingdom chose the left-hand path over the right, it might happen very soon.

Jago Moon was pacing back and forth in his agitation, and the tapping of his cane was becoming restless.

"Come and sit beside me and tell me what is troubling you," she said, patting the wooden pew as she settled herself upon it. She made an occasional gasp as she sought the position of least discomfort. *When did I get so old?* she wondered.

"I'm not worthy," said Moon.

"Nonsense," Mother Shepherd replied. "I'm a foolish old woman taking the weight off her legs. Who better to rest beside me than a stubborn old man? Now sit down and tell me what we're facing."

"I believe that the last Coin of Judas has surfaced," said Moon, and Mother Shepherd winced as fear grabbed her stomach and twisted hard.

"Are you sure?" she asked.

"I'm only surmising," said Moon, "but if it *is* the final Coin then we will all know soon enough."

"I need to know everything," said Mother Shepherd, her voice showing more calm than she felt. "Go back to the beginning."

"Lucy has just brought Nathaniel Kingdom to the eyrie," Moon explained.

"Benjamin's brother?"

"The same," Moon confirmed. "Apparently, Nathaniel and his father were returning from the docks when they spotted that they were being followed. They took shelter in one of the warehouses and hid there until they were sure that they were safe. When they finally returned to their lodgings they discovered that it had been ransacked and Ben was nowhere to be found."

"And where does the Coin fit in?"

"Nathaniel was in a desperate state when Lucy found him, he'd been searching for Ben all day. He told her that it was *his* fault Ben was missing. He said that if he hadn't spotted the Egyptian at the docks, then his father would never have gone over to speak with him and they would never have fallen into the grip of the Coin."

"I'm still not following."

"It seems that an Egyptian man gave Jonas a silver coin

which they hid under the floorboards in their room. Since their room had been torn apart Nathaniel assumes that the real owner came looking for it."

"That might be true," said Mother Shepherd, "but what makes you think that it's the Judas Coin?"

"Because of the way Nathaniel described it to Lucy. He told her that it was the most beautiful thing in the world and that since he had clapped eyes on it, he had been consumed with greed for it. Nathaniel said that he could hardly think of anything else, that he wanted it so much that it frightened him."

"It frightens me too," she said. She had hoped that she would not live to see the day that a Judas Coin was at large in London. One of those bloodstained pieces of silver was enough to turn a man from saint to sinner. How would a poor red-headed boy cope if it came within his grasp? "And do we know where Benjamin is?" she asked.

Moon shook his grizzled head. "We saw him go into the Under but no one has seen him emerge. We've got scouts watching the entrances that we are aware of, but you know as well as I do that there are hundreds of secret ways into that cesspit."

Mother Shepherd could hear the anger and fear churning together in her old friend's voice. "Have faith in Benjamin," she said. "He's young and foolish, but you told me yourself that he has a good heart. Just because he is with the Legion at the moment, it doesn't mean that he has joined them."

Moon made a scornful noise at the back of his throat and she chose to ignore it.

"If I sit down and dine with pigs, does that make me a pig too?" she asked.

"No, Great Mother," Moon conceded, "but you can't eat with pigs without getting covered in…"

"Shame?" she offered. "I take your point, old friend. We need to get Ben to a place of safety as soon as possible."

"Lucy has taken out a party to search for him," said Moon, happier now that he was talking about action, "and Josiah, and Ghost. I'll be setting out again too, as soon as we're done."

"I never doubted it," she said. "And what about Jonas Kingdom?"

"He's still out there looking for Ben, according to Nathaniel."

"Then we're doing everything we can," said Mother Shepherd. *I only pray that it is enough*, she added silently.

If Ben Kingdom made the wrong choice, if he listened to the Legion's lies and sided with them, then it wasn't only *his* soul that would be lost. It would begin with tens of thousands in London, and end with millions across the British Empire. And now one of the Judas Coins was at large and every eye in Hell would be drawn to it. If Ben was carrying the Coin *and* in the clutches of the Legion, what chance would one young boy have against such corrupting power?

And if he yielded to it, what chance did any of them have?

What have I gone and done this time? Ben asked himself, too late.

He was naked to the waist, and bound to a chair, hand and foot. Mickelwhite had taken a certain glee in making sure that the ropes bit deeply into his flesh and Ben had smiled at him as he did it, just to let Mickelwhite know that he would remember the favour and repay it one day. Meanwhile Munro, the hunchback, was somewhat gleefully pumping the fire back to life with a pair of bellows, while the other members of the strange band looked on with a mixture of excitement and fear.

Where Ben felt he might have been really unwise was that he had let them do this to him willingly, just to prove a point about not being scared.

He glanced over to where his shirt and tatty waistcoat

had been flung on the floor. Prior to the ceremony, Carter had taken the opportunity to search his pockets. And inside his boots. And socks.

Good old hat, thought Ben, as he saw it sitting quietly, drawing no attention to itself. *You keep that Coin nice and safe.*

The boys gathered around him then, jostling for a better position, and the uncomfortable heat of the fire was only partially responsible for the sweat that was starting to roll down his body.

At least Ruby Johnson had the decency to stand at the back, he thought. She hadn't said a word to him since she'd returned with Carter, and he hadn't spoken to her. It was clear to Ben that yesterday she had merely been acting under Carter's instruction; none of it had been real. She had suckered him into the Under and delivered him into Carter's hands. *Or* hand, *that should be*, thought Ben with a wry grin.

If only she had been upfront with him, he probably would have gone with her anyway. Damn it, why did she have to be so pretty?

When the coals were almost white, Carter took a branding iron and thrust it into the heart of the furnace. He let it rest there until it was glowing fiercely and then withdrew it slowly. Ben could feel the stinging heat of the brand but it didn't burn as ferociously as his anger towards the Watchers at that moment.

When Professor Carter had spoken about the war it had sounded like a game for gentlemen; we block their move, they take our pawn. But Mickelwhite and the boys had explained in no uncertain terms; the Watchers were evil. They told him the stories of the Witch Queen of Spies, about her cruelty and the sacrifices which she demanded for her spiteful god. And about her servant, the Weeping Man, who crawled the backstreets searching for lost children that he could bring to her as an offering.

"So, Benjamin," said Carter solemnly, "do you choose to join us of your own free will? Do you choose to be bound to us as a brother, to serve with us as a soldier?"

As Ben gazed at the smouldering tip of the branding iron, he saw clearly for the first time exactly who was to blame for the misfortunes that had been blighting his life. He thought of the wreckage of his room and the destruction of his few meagre possessions, and knew that it had been the work of the Watchers. He thought of Mr. Smutts and the fire which almost consumed him and knew that the bird-headed demons must have been summoned by the Witch Queen. He thought of little Molly Marbank, and shuddered at her fate in the clutches of the Weeping Man.

So why was there still a small nagging voice at the back of his mind, warning him that he was about to make a terrible mistake?

Ben thought of his brother, Nathaniel, prisoner of the Watchers and the doubt was silenced completely. "Ask me again!" Ben snapped.

"Do you choose to join the Legion of your own free will?"

"I do," said Ben firmly.

"To be one with us until death and beyond?"

"Till death and beyond."

Carter gave a nod and Mickelwhite took Ben's left hand and turned it over so that the palm was facing upwards. "This is going to sting," Mickelwhite hissed in his ear.

"Welcome to the Legion, Ben Kingdom," declared Claw Carter, pressing the branding iron into the soft flesh of his upturned hand.

Ben's world turned white with pain.

CHAPTER 24

THE MARK

"Hello, sleepyhead," said a gentle voice.

Ben opened one eye, unsure of where he was. Then he felt the raw throbbing of his left hand and it all came rushing back.

"*You*," said Ben, as he saw Ruby Johnson leaning over him. "I don't need your help." And to prove his point, he swung himself out of the bunk and promptly fell over.

"Take it easy," said Ruby softly, bending down to help him back up. "Nobody gets up quickly after they have taken the Mark."

Ben drew away from her touch as if she were a leper and struggled back onto the bed under his own steam.

They sat for a while in awkward silence.

"Why didn't you tell me that you were following Carter's orders when you brought me here?" asked Ben. "Why couldn't you have been honest with me instead of going through that whole ridiculous charade of being my friend?"

"I am your friend," she replied.

Ben winced as the pain in his palm really began to kick in.

"Here," she said, "let me take a look at that. I've got some salve here that will help the stinging."

Ben examined his hand for the first time. Burned into the skin was the image of a gauntlet, an armoured left fist. It hurt like anything, but it was a strong emblem, Ben thought. He took Ruby's pot of greasy ointment and tentatively began to rub it in, doing his best not to wince.

"We all have one," said Ruby, drawing off her glove to show her own hand. "It stands for strength and power," she explained. "It reminds us that wherever we are, we will always be part of the Legion." She trailed off slightly as she said it, making Ben wonder whether Ruby thought that was a good or bad thing.

Ben looked at the mark burned indelibly into his flesh. Despite the pain, he liked it. It reminded him of the tattoos that soldiers brought home from the wars; a sign of their brotherhood and adversities overcome.

"It shows that we belong," said Ben.

"And that we can never leave." There was definitely a sombre note in Ruby's voice now, but Ben didn't have time to question her because the barracks door opened and Mickelwhite strode in.

"Finally come back to the land of the living, have you?" said Mickelwhite.

"How long have I been asleep?" Ben asked Ruby.

"Hours," she said. "You've missed a whole day. It's getting dark outside again now."

Ben shook off his fatigue and forced himself to stand.

"Report to the armoury in ten minutes," snapped Mickelwhite. "Miss Johnson can fill you in on the way."

"Where are we going?" Ben asked, still disorientated.

"To rescue your brother," Mickelwhite answered, "and make the Watchers regret the day they ever heard the name 'Kingdom'."

Nathaniel Kingdom was standing on the roof of the Royal Albert Hall. A small pennant snapped in the wind, bearing the symbol of an open right hand; the sign of the Watchers.

There were lookouts high up on the dome itself, but

Nathaniel was with the rest of the encampment, safely on the lower tier below. The Watchers had made him welcome, and yet he was still a stranger in their strange land. He wandered around, trying to make sense of everything that the Watchers had told him. He still couldn't quite believe that the Watchers thought Ben was some sort of leader-in-waiting; if only they knew how often Ben was in trouble they would soon change their tune. What Nathaniel had no difficulty accepting was that Ben was in great danger if he was in the hands of the Legion. If even half of what the Watchers had explained to him about the Legion was true, then Ben was literally in the jaws of wickedness.

And then there was the Coin; a Judas Coin, Mr. Moon had thought. A Coin that had been steeped in blood down the ages and had the power to lead even the strongest will down the path to wickedness. If Ben was carrying the Coin, Nathaniel couldn't imagine the mental torture he must be going through.

Nathaniel's own head began to spin uncomfortably, and he didn't know whether it was shock or vertigo; either way he decided to stay well away from the edge. He had begun to pace restlessly again, when to his delight his eyes picked out a familiar face.

"Molly Marbank!" he shouted with delight, and went

to join the girl in her sheltered spot, in the lee of a wall.

Molly smiled at him. She was bundled up in a blanket to keep her warm and was slurping happily on a bowl of hot soup.

For a while they just sat. It was Molly who broke the silence.

"Why do you look so sad?" she asked sweetly. "Everyone is so kind here."

"I miss my family," he said. "My brother is lost and my pa has gone looking for him. I'm afraid that..." His voice cracked and hot tears welled in his eyes. "I'm afraid that Ben might die without knowing how much we love him. I know that I don't always treat Ben the way I should, I know that sometimes Pa can hardly bring himself to look at him..." Nathaniel couldn't have stopped the stream of words even if he'd wanted to. "It's Ben's hair," he continued, sniffing, "and his face and his uneven smile that me and Pa find so hard to cope with."

Molly looked confused.

"Ben looks just like our mother," Nathaniel explained. "Every time Ben smiles at Pa, it breaks his heart again."

Across the city of London, several Kingdoms had already been hastened to their deaths.

Grey Wing gave the tally, while Carter listened impassively.

Tobias Kingdom, a wig-maker, fell to his death from his upstairs window; Jonathan Kingdom, bookkeeper, drowned in his shaving bowl; Emma Kingdom, match-seller, died in flames. Samuel Kingdom, barrister-at-law, was stabbed in the back, before being dropped into the silent waters of St Katharine Docks.

"And you didn't eat them this time?" asked Carter.

Grey Wing made a shrugging motion with his vast shoulders. "Only the hearts," he said, "and some of the eyes."

"How positively restrained of you."

Carter had to admit that the Feathered Men had been busy. It was just a shame that all their interrogations had failed to provide so much as a single clue that would lead him closer to the Coin. He was convinced that if Ben *had* hidden the Coin, he would have let something slip by now; for all his qualities, the boy didn't seem to have a very tight rein on his tongue. That meant that either the Watchers *did* have the Coin, which Ben had maintained all along, or that Ben's father, possibly even his brother, was still in possession of that benighted piece of silver. However, in spite of the Feathered Men's efforts, Jonas and Nathaniel Kingdom seemed to have slipped off the face of the map.

The one consolation as far as he was concerned was that Benjamin Kingdom had taken the Mark. His left hand belonged to the Legion now. All that Carter needed to do to complete the boy's transformation was to ensure that his *soul* belonged to the Legion too.

Ben had so many questions that Ruby could hardly keep up with them.

He seemed to have forgiven her entirely for bringing him into the Under on false pretences and, for reasons that Ruby couldn't explain, that meant a lot to her.

"Can you tell me more about the Legion?" he asked.

She wasn't sure where to start. "I suppose the first thing you should understand is that not everyone in the Under is part of the Legion."

Ben showed his surprise. "So why do you let them live here?"

"When Alasdair Valentine began work on these tunnels, he saw a use for them straight away, making them far more valuable than the simple bolt-hole the King intended. Valentine imagined a place of sanctuary," she continued, "a place of refuge for all those who couldn't go running to the Crown or the Church. That principle holds true to this day."

"And so all the families down here, they're just refugees?"

Ruby nodded. "And escapees, or runaways or throwaways. All welcome. If someone wants to live among us, all they have to do is look after themselves and accept Legion rule."

Ben listened with rapt attention.

"Probably only a third of the denizens of the Under are Legionnaires. Of those who have taken the Mark, the bottom rank are serfs; that's what you are."

"Thanks," said Ben. "It's always nice to hear that you are the lowest of the low."

"Most of the young ragamuffins you see running around the place fall into that category too," Ruby went on. "Above them come certain young ladies and gentlemen such as Munro and Jimmy Dips who have shown themselves worthy and willing to work hard; they become squires. A squire will serve under a knight or a captain for a time, possibly years, learning more about the ways of our Order. Then come the knights, such as yours truly, organized into small brigades. There are reconnaissance brigades like ours, skirmish brigades and heavy-battle brigades. Each brigade is led by a captain – you've already met Captain Mickelwhite."

Ruby could see from his face exactly what Ben thought

of Captain Mickelwhite, as he marched along in front of them, leading the way to the armoury.

"Yes, well," said Ruby. She didn't always see eye to eye with Mickelwhite herself. "Be careful, Ben," she warned under her breath. "He's been watching you."

"Yes, I know," said Ben.

"No, you don't, Ben," she corrected him. She took his arm and allowed Mickelwhite's long stride to lengthen the distance between them. When the gap was wide enough, she spoke low and quickly. "None of us have ever known Professor Carter to initiate someone into the Legion so quickly. It's obvious that he thinks highly of you and Mickelwhite is jealous. You must be careful not to antagonize him."

She had meant it as a warning, but Ruby could see that it had had the opposite effect.

"It won't be long before I'm Captain and he'll have to be careful of me," said Ben, his eyes agleam.

CHAPTER 25

THE QUARTERMASTER

Mickelwhite brought them to a halt outside an impressive bronze door, inlaid with images of strange creatures: lions with wings, humans with the faces of animals, snakes that coiled round each other so that it was impossible to tell where one ended and the other began.

"Say nothing and follow my lead," Mickelwhite said curtly. "We are about to meet the Egyptian."

"And who's he when he's at home?" said Ben.

"He's the Legion quartermaster," Mickelwhite explained. "Before any brigade is sent out they have to report here to be equipped, and then return it all afterwards."

"So why mustn't I speak?" asked Ben.

"Because the last mouthy street boy who spoke out of turn to the Egyptian didn't come out alive," Mickelwhite replied.

The door opened with a sigh and the Egyptian appeared. He was a tall man, made taller by his blood-red hat, which Ben had heard called a "fez". He literally loomed over them, his head almost reaching the top of the door frame, his neck bent to observe them, like a heron watching fish. Widthways, the Egyptian was almost too narrow, and yet Benjamin suspected that he had a strong wiry build hidden beneath the folds of his purple silk robe, which was drawn at the waist with a tasselled belt.

It was impossible to guess the man's age but his skin was the brown of dead leaves and covered with a map of fine lines, especially around the eyes and across his broad, high forehead. The cheekbones were high as well, as if his skull was too close to the surface, leaving deep hollows in his cheeks and pits for his eyes.

Those eyes scared Ben more than anything. The coldest December night was not as cold as those two black pearls.

The Egyptian made a beckoning gesture and, without a word, the three young Legionnaires followed him into his domain. He led them down a flight of stone stairs into a cathedral-like chamber that two days ago Ben wouldn't have believed could exist beneath the pavements of London. The stonework was the most elaborate that he had seen so far on his journey into the Under. The pillars that held up the vaulted roof took the form of enormous figures, supporting the ceiling on their broad shoulders. Ben had seen similar columns on the front of the Egyptian Hall in Piccadilly, but that façade couldn't hold a candle to this.

The bodies were clearly human, both male and female, with loincloths and robes covering muscles and sinews of carved stone. But the heads were the heads of animals. Ben could make out a crocodile and a lion and other animals that he didn't have a name for; animals that hunted and killed. He looked at Ruby for explanation but all he received was a look that told him to hold his tongue.

As Ben went further into the chamber, a deep feeling stirred inside him. *I was born for this,* he thought.

Everywhere he looked his eyes fell on a new treasure. Not treasure in the way that some might think of it – not gold necklaces or caskets overflowing with jewels; those were treasures for old men or girls with heads full of silly dreams. The treasures that he saw here were for men of adventure. Men like Claw Carter. Men like him.

The walls were hung with an amazing array of equipment, some of which Ben recognized and some of which were as mysterious as its strange keeper. Instantly familiar were sturdy boots, cloaks, capes and trousers in every size, leather belts and harnesses, backpacks and coils of rope like long snakes waiting for the charmer's flute. On wooden mannequins hung breastplates, wrist cuffs, shin protectors: boys' stories of knights in armour come to life. Arranged neatly on tables and chests were bullseye lanterns with metal shutters, which could focus the light in a single beam; *the burglars' favourite*, thought Ben with a grin. Next to them sat chisels, files, hammers, pliers, crowbars and skeleton keys, designed to pick any lock in the right hands.

Then came some devices that were beyond Ben's understanding. Some were clockwork, with intricate cogs and wheels designed to roll with precision. Others were steam-powered, with copper boilers, valves and tubes, and gauges to measure the pressure. There were workbenches all around the chamber, strewn with the tools of a skilled man, and since the Egyptian appeared to be the only person permitted there, he had to be the craftsman who made all these implements as well as the quartermaster who accounted for them. Ben's mind reeled; this was incredible.

Then he saw the wall of weapons and his left hand throbbed with inner fire. *Yes*, he thought, *I'd like to have a go with those.*

There were crossbows on a rack – small powerful weapons that could be used with a single hand, like a pistol – and beside them a huge supply of crossbow bolts, some with sharp tips and others with fat weighted heads that Benjamin supposed could be used to knock someone out if fired with accuracy. He imagined himself with one of those pistols and made a mime of shooting...then he caught sight of Mickelwhite drawing a single finger across his throat and he let his imaginary crossbow fall to the floor.

Next to the crossbow pistols were other weapons: brass knuckles; knives of every conceivable size and shape; swords, pistols, rifles. And next to those was a collection of glass containers of various sizes – some small enough to fit into the palm of a hand, others that would require two strong men to carry them – all of them fitted with a length of fuse and filled with a grey dust that Ben guessed to be gunpowder. When the war against the Watchers came, the Legion would certainly be ready.

Wordlessly, the Egyptian bade them stand in a circle carved into the floor. Mickelwhite made the Legion salute, left fist on right shoulder, and then bowed, motioning for Ben and Ruby to do likewise. Ben found himself smiling broadly as he lowered his head: *What would the boys from Old Gravel Lane say if they could see me now?*

"This boy is a serf, My Lord," said Mickelwhite in his haughty tones. He pronounced the word "serf" in the way other men might refer to the contents of their chamber pot. "His name is Kingdom."

Ben might have been mistaken but he thought he saw a glimmer of recognition pass across the silent Egyptian's face and a low gurgle came from his throat. Then, with surprising speed, those long hands reached out and began to prod and pat Ben roughly.

"He's measuring you up," whispered Ruby. "Hold your arms out straight and spread your legs slightly."

Satisfied, the Egyptian moved soundlessly back and forth from his racks. Ben received metal wrist guards which fitted his forearms and could be used, he guessed, for blocking a Watcher attack, and similar shin protectors fitted to his legs, all of which were completely hidden beneath his clothes. He was given a new pair of boots, probably the best he had ever put on his feet, with sturdy ankle support, steel toecaps and solid grip. Then he was given a leather satchel, which he slung across his shoulder, a small canvas rucksack for his back, and a length of tightly coiled rope to be strung to his belt.

Ben could feel the excitement coursing through him. If only he had joined the Legion sooner, how different his life might have been.

The only slight disappointment was when, instead of being laden with bags and backpacks, Mickelwhite received a breastplate to wear beneath his shirt and one of the crossbow pistols, which sat snugly in a hidden holster below his left armpit where he could reach it at a moment's notice. "Privilege of rank, dear boy," Mickelwhite explained with a smirk.

Ruby rejected any armour but instead received a satchel which, when she looked inside it made her eyes light up. Knowing her skills as a thief, Ben guessed that it contained the tools of her trade.

Ben's own abilities in that direction were improving too. While the Egyptian had his back turned, Ben's nimble left hand sneaked out and claimed a collapsible brass telescope; he had always fancied one of those. He thought of the silver Coin then, still safe in its hiding place in his hatband. It was strange; it was almost as if since he found the Coin stealing had become so much easier.

When the Egyptian had provided them with everything that he was prepared to give, he gave them a small nod to show that they were dismissed. They saluted and made for the stairs. As an afterthought, Ben called over his shoulder: "Thanks, mate!"

The Egyptian made a dark noise, halfway between a bark and a snarl.

"I told you to say nothing!" Mickelwhite snapped when they were back in the corridor, the bronze door firmly shut.

"That noise he made," said Ben. "What's wrong with him?"

"Haven't you got it yet?" Mickelwhite pushed his face up close to Ben's, his nostrils flaring. "The Legion is made up of people who don't fit in up there." He jerked his finger towards the roof and the rest of London beyond. "Everyone in the Under has a history and if someone doesn't tell you, then it's not your place to ask."

"But if he's ill—"

Mickelwhite cut him off. "He's not sick."

"So why can't he speak then?"

"It's his punishment for a crime he committed a long time ago," said Ruby.

"What did he do?"

"Nobody knows," said Mickelwhite. "But it must have been serious because they cut out his tongue as his just reward."

Ben went white. Old Gravel Lane was filled with rough sorts and too many scoundrels to count, but the Under was a different world entirely.

Ruby's words came back to haunt him.

All welcome.

222

CHAPTER 26

HERO OF
THE LEGION

The rescue party was assembled in the tunnel at the foot of an iron ladder.

It was a simple enough plan. They would find a Watcher, track them back to their camp, and spring Nathaniel from captivity. The main difficulty that Mickelwhite had outlined was that the Watchers changed the location of their camp every night, plus they had the advantage of knowing all the secret paths across the roof of the city.

Ben also had his own private concerns. He had not forgotten the Weeping Man, or the sword that hung at his side.

Alexander Valentine would not be joining them; the weakness in his lungs was very bad that night. Squire Munro would not be coming either. His shape, his lack of agility and his general flatulence all limited his ability in the field. He said farewell with a solemn bow and a slight belch. That left six of them: Captain Mickelwhite, Hans Schulman, John Bedlam, Jimmy Dips, Ruby and Ben himself.

This close to the surface, the Legion were always on guard, and Ben could feel the tension that hung around their shoulders, as cold and heavy as damp wool. Mickelwhite waited for absolute silence before he sent Jimmy Dips scampering up the ladder to open the trapdoor in the roof. The whereabouts of the entrances to the Under were among the most fiercely protected secrets of the Legion. Ruby had told Ben that more than once an entrance had had to be sealed up, or even whole sections of tunnel abandoned, just because a Legionnaire had been careless and allowed themselves to be seen. Captain Mickelwhite was taking no chances.

Jimmy climbed carefully, making sure that his boots landed softly on the rungs. Then he lifted the stone slab a tiny fraction and peered out into the night with his rat-pink eyes. Satisfied that no one was about, Jimmy lifted the slab higher and cast around with his bullseye lantern, its tight narrow beam reaching out into the dark.

"All clear," he whispered and they followed him up the ladder, their lips firmly buttoned shut, until they were all standing in the enclosed darkness of a cellar.

The armour on Ben's wrists and shins felt heavy, and the pack on his back was even worse. Mickelwhite had taken the opportunity to fill it with a dozen more items, each of which he declared to be invaluable for the mission ahead. Ben was far from convinced, especially when he saw the sly looks that Mickelwhite and his knights exchanged with each additional burden that they insisted he carry for them.

He knew that the captain and Valentine in particular both looked down their noses at him. He was scum to them: some poor boy from the East End, not fit to mix with the likes of them. *They'd better watch out*, Ben thought with a smile. *Scum has a habit of rising to the top of the pond*. When he'd been sure no one was looking, he had switched the silver Coin from his hatband to his pocket, and he touched it now for comfort. *My time will come.*

Carefully, so as not to make a sound, Jimmy Dips lowered the trapdoor back into place, and Ben was surprised to see that an old chair and a square of carpet were fixed to the door so that when it was closed there was no sign that it had even been there. Jimmy opened the shutters on the lantern a little wider to illuminate the room and Ben saw that they were in a basement, filled with old tea chests and junk. There wasn't even the slightest clue that they were standing at an entrance to an underground world.

No, that wasn't quite true. Ben looked closer and saw a symbol on the chair, no bigger than a farthing: the sign of the gauntleted fist. Ben smiled to himself; one day all the secrets of the Legion would be his.

"The Hag is the wickedest woman in London," Mickelwhite explained. "All she wants to do is to ensnare the weak-minded and bind them to her will."

Ben wasn't really listening. They had been trawling the snowbound streets for almost two hours without even a sniff of the Watchers. They were never going to find Nathaniel at this rate.

Ben's backpack felt as if Mickelwhite had slipped an anvil into it while he wasn't looking; Ben knew that his shoulders were red and raw under the straps. The armour that had been so exciting to put on was nothing more than another deadweight to carry, and with their glorious captain leading them round in circles, the whole expedition was coming to nothing.

If Mickelwhite was the best that the Legion had to offer, then it would take him no time to rise through the ranks, Ben thought. And why stop at captain? Ben would be a knight commander, just like Claw Carter, and then Mickelwhite would be the one doing the saluting and carrying the bags.

On top of that, Ben still had the Roman Coin. He hadn't forgotten that Ruby had been sniffing for it when they were in the laundry together, and he could tell from Carter's icy calm when he first mentioned it in his study that the professor was keen to have it for himself. Surreptitiously, Ben's fingers rubbed its smooth surface where it lay hidden in his pocket and he thrilled to the touch.

"Are you alright?" Ruby asked quietly.

"What's it to you?" he snapped back.

She was obviously envious of him too, just like Mickelwhite. They all wanted to be Claw Carter's favourite, they all wanted his Coin. Well, they would have to go on wanting. Ben Kingdom had waited long enough for his chance, and now that it had finally come his way, he wasn't sharing it with anyone. He would reveal the Coin when he was good and ready, at precisely the right moment for maximum impact and personal glory.

Benjamin Kingdom, the hero of the Legion.

He caught Ruby's eye to show her how glad he was that she had brought him into the Under. But for some inexplicable reason, the expression she gave him in return was filled with sadness.

DAY FIVE
24TH DECEMBER -
CHRISTMAS EVE, 1891

CHAPTER 27

THE HUMAN HEART

Standing there on the rooftop at midnight, Molly Marbank felt very grown up indeed.

Josiah was brilliant, she thought. He let her stay up way past her bedtime and he was teaching her how to be a Watcher too. She had an extending ladder folded tight in her backpack, along with some supplies for the night and her own set of hand hooks for using on the slide ropes. She was getting quite good at running in her skyboots, even though she said it herself, although she wasn't brave enough to try a jump on her own yet.

She was also making some new friends.

Molly had met all sorts of people in the Watchers.

There was a blind man called Mr. Moon who was quite scary, although the others said he was fine once you got to know him. And there was a lovely old lady who looked after them all, and she was called Mother Shepherd, although Molly had called her "Granny" once by accident and everyone laughed. Just having them around made everyone feel safe.

And there were the others too, of course, standing side by side with her now on the roof tiles, London unaware below them: Josiah, the great and mighty Weeping Man; Lucy Lambert, a girl with a fiery temper, probably explained by the angry scar that she tried so hard to hide; Ghost, the African boy who never spoke a word and got his name because he moved so silently; and Nathaniel, her new big brother.

Molly smiled. What would anyone think if they could see them now?

"Watcher filth," said Mickelwhite.

It was the stroke of midnight when they spotted them. Stark silhouettes against the night sky. Five spies hiding among the chimneys.

"Let's get 'em," hissed John Bedlam through gritted teeth.

Ben wasn't sure whether Bedlam was filled with anger or frozen to the marrow. Chances were it was a bit of both. He knew that he was freezing cold and pretty cheesed off himself. They had been skulking around in the backstreets for what felt like ages, waiting for a glimpse of their enemies. It had got boring quicker than he'd expected. All soldiers were restless when they weren't fighting, he supposed.

Plus he was getting a terrible crick in the back of his neck.

Ben was temporarily stunned when they finally found their foe. It was like looking into a mirror. The Watchers were just another gang of raggedy girls and boys. Although the Watchers had better jackets, he noted with envy.

They were too far away to make out their faces. All Ben could tell for certain was that there were four small childlike Watchers and a fifth, larger adult one. Pulling out the telescope he had stolen earlier, Ben put it to his eye to confirm his fear. There was no mistaking that outline. The long coat. The tall hat. It was a man that he had hoped never to see again. A man in black who carried a sword and cried in the night.

"It's the Weeping Man," said Ben quietly.

"Then we'll have to be especially careful not to be seen," said Mickelwhite, "but the plan remains the same.

We follow them at a distance, find out where their base is tonight, then return to the Under for reinforcements."

"And then we come back and start smashing heads," said Bedlam.

"And rescue my brother," Ben added.

"That too," said Bedlam with markedly less enthusiasm.

Mickelwhite split them into three groups, to increase their chances of tracking the Watchers, he said. Ben guessed the real reason though: Mickelwhite couldn't stand the sight of him.

Jimmy Dips and Mickelwhite went one way, Schulman and Bedlam another, leaving Ben and Ruby Johnson alone.

"So," said Ben, not certain where he stood with Ruby any more.

"So," said Ruby.

"Are you ready for this?" asked Ben.

"As ready as I'll ever be," Ruby replied.

"Fine," said Ben.

"Fine," said Ruby. "Let's go."

Lucy spotted them first. "Movement, down there!"

"Quick," said Nathaniel Kingdom, taking out his rope ladder and fixing it to the guttering with a swift sailor's knot that he'd learned at the docks. "It could be him," he said with excitement. Ghost nodded his agreement, his beautiful eyes bright in his dark face.

"I'll go first," said Lucy, swinging herself out over the edge of the roof, unmoved by either the height or what she might be facing when she reached the bottom.

Only Molly Marbank hesitated, seeing Josiah's expression. "What are you thinking?" she asked him.

Josiah closed his eyes before answering. "Nathaniel believes that one word from him will be enough to bring his brother over from the side of darkness and into the light."

"But that's good, isn't it?" Molly was confused. "Don't *you* want Benjamin to join the Watchers?"

"Yes, it is what I want," said Josiah. "More than anything. But Nathaniel has got his hopes up and I fear he might be terribly disappointed." The Weeping Man sighed. "The human heart can be so difficult to predict."

Molly still didn't understand. "But it's such an easy choice," she said. "I came straight away, didn't I?"

Josiah smiled at her and she felt a warm glow in her young heart. "Yes, you did, little one," he said.

"And what about you?" she asked excitedly. "Was it a difficult choice for you?"

"No," Josiah replied. "But you know that my heart is not human at all."

For some reason, Ruby had stopped running.

Ben could see her a short way ahead of him, standing stock-still at the junction of three roads. From her expression, he guessed that she had found the Watchers. Or more likely the Watchers had found her.

A flutter of movement on the edge of his vision drew his eyes up to a chimney stack, three storeys above the ground. There was a rope tied around it and stretched out taut across the street to the two-storey houses on the other side. The shadowy movement came again, followed by a scuffing sound as spiked boots struck the tiles. As Ben stared, a Watcher took a running leap into the air and, with the fluidity of motion born of practice and great bravery, flung a small metal hook around the rope and clung to it with both hands. With the rushing noise of a sail unfurling, the Watcher flew over Ben's head, riding down the rope to land, running, on the opposite rooftop.

Suddenly Watchers seemed to be appearing from all sides. Rope ladders clattered to the ground and figures dropped down them soundlessly, all dressed in the Watcher uniform of long coats and aviators' goggles, faces hidden beneath scarves. They were only street kids like him, Ben reminded himself, but he was outnumbered. He wished that he had stolen something more useful from the Egyptian, like a cudgel so he could defend himself. *What am I going to do with a telescope? Magnify them to death?*

The Watchers regarded him coldly. Mickelwhite had led him to believe that the Watchers were cowards who would run rather than stand and fight. This lot seemed intent on proving Mickelwhite wrong, however, and as much as Ben would enjoy his beloved captain being mistaken, he was disappointed that he was going to have to take a beating just to prove a point.

"Ruby!" he shouted – there was nothing to be gained by being quiet any more. "Come on," he urged her. "We can hold them off together while we wait for reinforcements."

Ruby came running towards him then, her mouth set in a hard line. He knew that he could rely upon her. In seconds she was beside him. Ben flashed her a quick smile, but it fell completely from his face as Ruby reached inside her jacket and withdrew a long, thin knife.

Blimey, thought Ben, *this could turn nasty.*

The Watchers began to move in and Ben positioned himself so that he and Ruby were back to back.

"We can take 'em," he said, more boastfully than

truthfully, but it felt like the right thing to say. "You and me."

"I'm sorry," said Ruby. Her words scared him more than anything else; he had never heard her sound so defeated.

"Don't be sorry," he said, still trying to have enough bravado for the pair of them. "There's no one I'd rather have beside me."

"No. You don't understand. I'm sorry for this," said Ruby as she grabbed him in a headlock from behind and held the tip of the knife hard between his ribs, ready to pierce his heart.

"This is Benjamin Kingdom!" she shouted to the Watchers. "If you want him to live, give me the Judas Coin!"

CHAPTER 28

THE FACE OF THE ENEMY

F or a long cold second, nobody moved.

And then it seemed as if everybody did.

Ben grasped Ruby's knife hand and wrenched it away. Strangely, she hardly put up any resistance at all, as if the spirit had already gone out of her. He knew that the Judas Coin could only be the piece of silver that he had been clinging to as if his life depended on it. What he didn't know was why everyone wanted it so badly. Ben didn't have time to think about that now though, because the Watchers fell on both of them in a blur.

A Watcher with a shaven head and ebony skin charged at Ruby. He pounced like a panther and sent her staggering back, the knife falling from her hand and skittering across the cobbles. At the same time, another Watcher rushed in close to Ben and, with a sweeping kick, hooked his legs out from under him. Ben fell flat on his back and felt the air knocked from his lungs as the Watcher leaped on him and pinned him down.

Everything was going too fast for Ben. He was shocked that Ruby had sold him out – he'd never seen it coming – but he could be glad at least that she had shown her true colours before he'd started to really like her. *Two-faced, money-grabbing back-stabber,* he thought angrily. Life would be so much easier without a girl like Ruby around. In the meantime, he had other things to worry about. The Watcher that was holding him down was very light, but strong with it. Their knees were pressed deep into his shoulders, preventing him from lifting himself off the floor, while their small hands held Ben's arms back above his head.

For a moment Ben thought that he had been beaten by a child younger than him, but when he looked more closely he could see that it was worse than that: he'd been thrown to the floor and was being pinned down by a *girl*. He bucked wildly in an attempt to knock her off, but to his frustration she stayed on him as if she were breaking in a troublesome pony.

"Don't struggle," she said. "You'll hurt yourself."

The girl had honey-coloured hair that stirred constantly around her face in the night air. A small mouth, set in a determined line. One clear blue eye; just the one, Ben couldn't help but notice. The other was hidden beneath an eyepatch that surely had something to do with the scar that ran from her hairline, disappeared beneath the patch, and then re-emerged to make the full journey down her pale cheek.

He became aware of heavy bootsteps, crunching across the cobbles towards him, coming to a halt when they arrived at Ben's head.

This night keeps getting better and better, he thought as he looked up and braced himself for a kicking.

The figure gazing down at him was clearly a Watcher, from the spiked boots to the long coat and brass goggles; all the accoutrements of the opposing army…except for the face.

"Hello, Ben," said a familiar voice, "I've been looking for you."

Part of Ben had started to believe that he might never see his family again, so finding Nathaniel standing in front of him sent such a wave of relief surging through Ben that he could hardly contain it.

At a signal from Nathaniel, the girl released Ben and he

picked himself up off the floor. Ruby was nowhere to be seen. *Good riddance to bad rubbish,* he thought angrily; although he couldn't help wondering if she had managed to get away to safety.

He looked at his brother.

For that instant, there was only the two of them in the whole of London. He could hear shouts and scuffles from the nearby alleys as Mickelwhite and the others clashed with the Watchers. But none of it mattered.

"Nathaniel," said Ben quietly.

Then, with a warmth that caught Ben totally off guard, Nathaniel threw his arms around him and hugged him. Ben saw something in Nathaniel's face that he had never seen there so clearly before. He saw love.

A hundred questions rushed to Ben's mind. *Where've you been? Are you hurt? Were you there when the room was destroyed? Are the Watchers keeping you prisoner?* And biggest of all: *Do you know where Pa is?*

The expression in Nathaniel's eyes was enough for Ben to boil all of those thoughts down into three small words. He leaned forward to embrace Nathaniel again and whispered into his ear. "Come with me!"

"No," said Nathaniel. "Don't be stupid, Ben. *You* come with *me.* Quick!" he added. "The Watchers are waiting for you."

Ben was confused. First Ruby had sold him out. And now Nathaniel was dressed as the enemy and asking him to go over to the other camp.

When Ben had been convinced that his brother was a prisoner of the Watchers everything had seemed so simple, but the fact that Nathaniel was with them willingly troubled him. For all that their father preferred Nathaniel, Ben had always believed that he wasn't that different to his big brother. How could they end up on opposite sides in this war?

So much had happened in the last few days that he didn't know who to believe any more.

"Come on, Ben," Nathaniel urged, as he headed back towards a rope ladder and prepared to climb it. "We haven't got time to hang around."

Nathaniel was right on that account, of course; Ben could hear Mickelwhite and Bedlam approaching. It was time to choose sides.

Ben's feet remained rooted until the youngest Watcher stepped forward from the shadows and settled the matter for him. He hadn't really given her much thought until now; she was such a little scrap of a thing. But as she moved closer and held out her hand Ben remembered the last time he had seen those frail fingers.

"Molly!" he declared, and she responded with a

gap-toothed smile. She looked happy and well-fed, Ben thought. And she definitely wasn't dead. So that could mean only one thing – the Weeping Man was not a killer after all.

And the Legion were full of lies.

"I'm coming, Nathaniel," Ben yelled, running to the foot of the ladder that his brother was already climbing. For a second he stood amazed as all the Watchers, little Molly Marbank included, ascended up their own ropes as swiftly as rats in the rigging. Only Nathaniel remained, hanging back and waiting for Ben.

Ben's face felt funny and he had to touch his mouth before he recognized what was wrong. He was smiling again; a huge lopsided grin that he couldn't contain.

I was getting bored of the Legion, anyway, he thought as he took the rope ladder in his hands and prepared to follow Nathaniel up onto the rooftop.

"Quickly!" Nathaniel insisted again. "We haven't got time to play games, Ben, what are you waiting for? You haven't given them Pa's coin have you?"

Ben froze. The smile dead on his lips.

All his peace abandoned him and in its place came a surge of pure fury.

The Coin!

You just want my Coin!

Ferociously, without any clear thought except anger, Ben started to climb after his brother, hand over fist.

We'll see about that!

London had changed since Lucy had first heard the name Ben Kingdom. She could sense it deep within her and other Watchers had reported it too: darkness was on the rise. It wasn't anything that she could put her finger on, more a subtle shift in the atmosphere. In the streets, in the drinking houses, in the factories, in rich houses and poor, tensions were becoming frayed, like wire that had been drawn too taut and was ready to snap. Rows were breaking out across the city: husband versus wife, father versus son, friend against friend. It was the presence of the Coin, she had no doubt; Watcher history taught that those cursed pieces of silver were always accompanied by bloodshed. First came the jealousy, then resentment, then the murderous rage.

One thing was for certain, Lucy realized as she looked back over her shoulder – the Legion were becoming bolder. You either had to be very foolhardy or very brave to follow the Watchers up onto the rooftops, but that was exactly what this brigade was doing now. *I just pray that they don't catch up with us*, Lucy thought, as she bounded across the tiles.

Lucy was a good enough fighter. Mr. Moon had taught her well but that didn't stop the swell of fear in her belly. She wasn't afraid for herself – it was Molly she was scared for. It had been a mistake to let her come with them at all – she should've been safely tucked up at the eyrie – but what was done was done. Lucy hung back and drew a small length of pipe from her backpack. She gave a quick flick of her wrist and the metal tube telescoped out until she was holding a quarterstaff, which she spun about her, cutting through the air. With her good eye, she signalled to Ghost, who drew out his crossbow and began to lay down a covering fire.

Nathaniel was still lagging behind them. He was holding them back but it was hardly his fault. He hadn't had time to get used to his skyboots and so he wasn't much quicker than the Legion as he staggered and slipped across the roof.

Ghost crouched and sent another bolt speeding towards the pursuing Legionnaires. The trouble was that he wouldn't hit any of them, Lucy knew. Unless there were no other options, Ghost wouldn't ever shoot to kill. Ghost was a true Watcher, and violence was not the Watcher way.

Ahead of them Josiah was picking the safest path for their escape, while Molly clung to his hand for dear life.

Every now and then the little girl looked up at the Weeping Man, and Lucy could see the way that he smiled down at her, with no trace of fear or panic on his beautiful face. Which was more than could be said for Nathaniel Kingdom. Nathaniel appeared terrified as he stumbled and skittered over the slates towards them.

And finally came Ben Kingdom, running with determination. Falling, picking himself up. Running again.

Perhaps Nathaniel had been able to persuade him after all?

Ben was going to kill him.

But he would have to catch Nathaniel first.

In spite of the blood pounding inside his head Ben was aware that he wasn't alone on the roof. On the periphery of his vision he could see Hans Schulman making heavy weather of a rope ladder and Jimmy Dips stuck halfway up a drainpipe, apparently unable to go up or down. Ruby Johnson was nowhere to be seen. Only Mickelwhite and Bedlam had made it up onto the roof tiles and both were following in hard pursuit.

Ben had to admit that the Watchers were incredible, racing away with the sure-footedness of mountain goats.

Some gaps they simply jumped, giving them no more thought then he did to jumping a puddle. To cross the bigger drops, Ben could see that the Watchers used ladders or planks which they must have hidden on the roofs in advance, only putting them out to span the gaps when they needed to, and then pulling the bridge across after them once they were on the other side.

But the most impressive thing was the way that they moved. They seemed to leap with such ease, using gutters and walls as springboards, giving the impression that they were skipping away rather than fleeing for their lives. Ben did his best to follow his brother, but he had to think about each step. Twice he had slipped, sending broken slates spinning into the darkness.

Mickelwhite, for all his lankiness, had a certain grace and his long legs were closing the gap. John Bedlam, on the other hand, who possessed not one single ounce of poise or elegance, was making ground on the fleeing Watchers based solely on his desire to start a fight.

Ben studied the Watchers as he ran, copying what they did as best he could. He was beginning to work out the surest way to plant his feet on the roof tiles, and had learned that the quickest path was along the ridge at the apex of a roof; so long as he didn't look down. He dumped his bags and rid himself of his armour as he ran, stripping off anything that would slow him.

He was gaining on Nathaniel and his entire left arm throbbed in anticipation.

Nathaniel wanted to steal his Coin.

He would pay for that.

CHAPTER 29

THE DROP

Mickelwhite was gone. Ben couldn't see him any more. He had either come to a gap he couldn't cross or fallen to his death; Ben wasn't much bothered which. John Bedlam was still tearing along with no thought for his own safety and was running a parallel course to Ben. A crossbow bolt struck a chimney next to Bedlam's head and the pot exploded into a thousand shards; he staggered but didn't slow.

Gradually, their paths began to converge until Ben and Bedlam both dropped down onto a welcome stretch of flat roof and were running side by side. The Watchers were in sight, Nathaniel in the rear, and both boys dug into their last reserves and started to sprint.

The African Watcher levelled his crossbow pistol again. The bolt sliced through the air towards them and Ben instinctively flicked out with his left hand and batted it away. Another innocent chimney pot was shattered to pieces beside him and peppered his face with splinters. Ben touched his fingers to his cheek and they came away kissed with blood, black in the moonlight.

He took the Coin out of his pocket with his left hand and clenched it so tightly in his fist that his veins stood proud.

Josiah didn't even slow as he thundered towards the edge of the roof with Molly tucked under his arm. When he reached the dead drop, he leaped high into the air, his feet continuing to pedal furiously until he landed safely on the next flat roof over, fifteen feet away. In a single fluid move he retrieved a Watcher ladder from its hiding place and, anchoring one end against his upraised foot, he lowered the ladder down until it bridged the wide gap.

Lucy crossed the ladder towards him, running over the rungs, her honey-coloured hair like a halo in the cold light of the moon. Then came Ghost, firing his last bolt as a warning across their pursuers' path.

Nathaniel Kingdom made it as far as the middle of the

ladder and then paused, his hand outstretched behind him. Lucy saw something close to desperation on his face.

"Come on," Nathaniel urged his brother. "Quickly!"

The edge of the building was less than ten feet away from Ben and in mere moments he would be out on the ladder too. Nathaniel was waiting for him there, with his hand still outstretched for the Coin.

Behind Ben was John Bedlam, grinning like a lunatic. They both put on a final spurt.

It was only when he and Bedlam were neck and neck that it occurred to Ben that they were running full tilt towards a four-storey drop and going too fast to stop. His only hope, he realized, was to make the ladder first. He glanced at Bedlam's mad eyes and knew that they both had the same idea.

Benjamin felt sick.

He could feel each of his footfalls as he thundered towards open air, his legs beginning to buckle. His lungs were made of fire; there was no strength left in him. But he simply could not stop now.

Somehow, he managed to ease himself a hair's breadth in front of Bedlam and then he dived for the ladder, throwing himself towards it full length. He hit it heavily, awkwardly, the wood slamming against him. For a fraction of a second he found himself lying with his face between the rungs, staring down at the pavement and the death that waited for him there. Then Bedlam landed behind him, half on top of him, and with such force that the vibrations threatened to shake them both off. The wood bowed dangerously and Ben's stomach clenched.

And then, to Ben's absolute horror, the ladder slipped from the edge of the roof, leaving him and Bedlam both clutching thin air.

Lucy was convinced that she was about to watch both Kingdom brothers fall.

When Ben and the other Legionnaire had flung themselves onto the flimsy ladder-bridge, they had dislodged their end and so now it was only supported on the Watchers' side. She and Ghost pushed down on their end with all their might, desperate to keep it suspended, but it was surely only a matter of time. Lucy could feel her arms shuddering with the effort. Ghost's beautiful eyes met hers, his thick arms bulging beneath his Watcher greatcoat. If the ladder went now, it would drag them both with it. Quickly Josiah stepped in to help take the strain and even Molly added her weight, such as it was.

Stuck in the middle of the ladder, Nathaniel had been cast off balance by the impact and tipped over the side, only managing to grab a hold by some miracle. Now he was hanging precariously underneath, his teeth clenched as he tried to find the strength to drag himself back up.

Lucy gave Josiah and Ghost a nod. "One, two, three," she breathed, and on the last count they all heaved together and began to haul the ladder to safety; slow inch by slow inch.

She could see Ben swinging from the ladder too, with the other boy hanging desperately from Ben's legs. Ben looked tortured, Lucy thought. Not cocky or clever. Just a boy in torment.

Hang on, Ben Kingdom!

Ben had never known pain like it. He wouldn't have been surprised if his arms were ripped from their sockets. His fingers were slick with sweat and his grip was failing.

Bedlam was swinging below him, trying to get a hold on Ben's belt, but slipping all the time. Ben tried to get a better grip, but their combined weight was too much for him.

He still had the Coin though. He could feel it in his left hand, held there by two fingers, while he tried to save his life with the other three.

"Try not to struggle," he snarled down at Bedlam, who was kicking out wildly with his legs. "You'll have us both off, you idiot!"

The ladder jerked again as the Watchers tried desperately to drag it over to their side to rescue their comrade. Ben could see his brother, hanging only a few feet away. Bedlam continued to thrash, his grasp sliding down to Ben's thighs, his nails digging into Ben's legs through the rough wool of his trousers. Ben braced himself for the moment when it became too much strain to bear and gravity had her way with the lot of them.

Drop the Coin, said a voice inside his head that was not his own. *It will pull you down*, the voice warned. *Let it go.*

Ben knew that his strength was failing. It made sense to drop the stupid thing and use all his might to hold on. But it never felt like a simple choice when it came to the Coin.

Bedlam gave a strangled gasp and fell two more feet until he was hanging from Ben's ankles. Ben wasn't sure how much longer he could hold on for: ten seconds? Five?

Perhaps if he could somehow get the Coin into his mouth and hold it there, he could use two hands to save them both? Perhaps if he found the strength, he could help Nathaniel too?

Or perhaps he could shake John Bedlam off and just save himself?

CHAPTER 30

FALLING

Ben had no idea where that last thought had come from and it revolted him; although not enough for him to let the Coin fall from his fingers.

His muscles were screaming. Beneath him, John Bedlam was screaming. On the other end of the ladder, the Watchers were screaming.

Then another scream rang out, so pure and clear that it silenced the rest of the world. Time slowed down, just as it had the first time that Ben met the Weeping Man. Three seconds passed as slowly as a hundred years.

One.

He saw his brother Nathaniel lose his grip on the

ladder and begin his journey to the waiting pavement below. And in that moment, Benjamin realized that he didn't want Nathaniel to die. He didn't hate him any more; he wasn't even cross with him. He wanted to be friends with his brother again and to find their father together. But the cobblestones of London wouldn't allow that. This is how it would end for Nathaniel. Flesh on rock, bone on stone.

Two.

With Nathaniel's weight suddenly removed, the ladder made a shuddering lurch that almost wrenched Ben's arms from their sockets. John Bedlam hung round his legs like an albatross, slowly clawing his way back up.

"Help me," Bedlam hissed in between groans, but there was nothing that Ben could do.

Three.

In a blur, something rushed past them both. A flash of purest white, accompanied by the beating of two enormous wings.

It was the Weeping Man.

He was an angel.

Ben had no other way to describe what his eyes were seeing.

Beneath that long black coat, he had been hiding a massive pair of wings. Wings the colour of clean linen, that carried the Weeping Man in a soaring arc; first up and then straight down, dropping like a hawk towards the ground.

And before Nathaniel hit the floor, before the cobbles could steal his life away, the Weeping Man swooped in and caught him in his arms. Then, while Ben looked on helplessly, the angel carried his brother skyward, high up above the clouds.

Ben felt numb.

If Nathaniel is fighting on the side of the angels, then whose side was I on?

And now, even though their comrade was safe, the remaining Watchers continued to pull the ladder to the safety of the other side. Ben didn't understand why they would choose to show mercy on two Legionnaires when it made more sense to let them fall. It didn't match with their description as the enemy. More lies that Carter had fed him, he realized.

But whatever their reasons, he was glad they were acting the way they were. Every tendon, every fibre of muscle in his arms was in agony. If he could just hang on until the Watchers dragged him to safety…

"Keep still," Ben snarled, as Bedlam continued to climb up Ben's body. "We're nearly safe now."

"No thanks to you," Bedlam replied.

The Watchers didn't speak as they hauled the ladder the last few yards and then dragged Ben and Bedlam up onto the roof. Neither of the boys had the strength to do anything except lie motionless on their backs, glad to be alive.

The Watcher girl came to stand over Ben. She looked down at him with something close to compassion, her expression a strange contrast with her blood-red scar and eyepatch.

"Come with us," she said, holding out her hand to help him up.

There was something in her voice that meant Ben knew he could trust her, and his fingers stretched out for hers.

Suddenly, as he watched, her face became a mask of pain. Her hand snatched away from his to clasp her own shoulder. She gazed at her fingers, confused by the blood that she found there. Ben's eyes looked back to the building opposite. Mickelwhite levelled his crossbow again.

Even then, she hesitated.

Schulman and Dips joined their captain with weapons of their own.

Bedlam staggered to his feet and made a lunge for the girl.

"I've been waiting a long time for this, beautiful," Bedlam snarled.

Ben leaped between the Legionnaire and the Watcher. "Go," he told the girl. "*Go!*"

She ran, following the other Watchers across the rooftops and away.

Ben grinned; he couldn't help it.

"What d'you do that for?" growled Bedlam and, before Ben could answer, he swung a punch which caught Ben square on the jaw, slamming his head back.

"Not bad," Ben confessed, giving his chin a rub and testing his teeth with his tongue to check for any wobblers. "Now, would you like to find out how a boy punches?"

Ruby was fed up with boys and all their stupid games.

She left them to it, making her own way back into the Under, choosing the quiet paths and forgotten tunnels so that she could be alone with her thoughts.

The Legion was the only family that she had ever known, but that didn't mean that she had to love them, did it? Part of her wanted nothing more to do with them, but she knew that they didn't take kindly to people leaving. Deserters were hunted down. The lucky ones got to live out the rest of their days as slaves, never seeing the light of day again. The less fortunate ones were given to the Feathered Men – as playthings.

She had failed Claw Carter and now she would have to face the music for that. He was no closer to the Coin, and he wouldn't take that news kindly.

But far worse was the way that Benjamin had looked at her.

She had seen in his eyes that everything had changed between them. She didn't blame him, of course; if he had held a knife to her ribs, she would never speak to him again.

Benjamin Kingdom was arrogant, stupid and thoroughly irritating…and so it came as a nasty surprise to Ruby that the thought of never being annoyed by him again was almost enough to put a tear in her big green eyes.

Ben didn't know where the anger came from.

He had got into scraps before but he had never beaten someone the way he laid into John Bedlam. It was almost as if he had no control over his body. His left hand had a life all of its own, existing solely for the purpose of raining blow upon blow on the other boy.

Then he remembered the Coin nestled safely back in his pocket, and it all clicked into place: Bedlam wanted it for himself, that must be it.

Well, he can't have it, thought Ben, and he began punching him again.

Bedlam had stopped fighting a few moments ago and was simply lying there, absorbing punches. Part of Ben was screaming for him to stop, although he couldn't make the message extend to his fist.

When Ben realized that Mickelwhite was standing over him, it actually came as a relief. The decision to stop was taken out of his hands by a swift cudgel blow to the back of his head.

And the darkness that came with it was a welcome escape.

CHAPTER 31

THE VERY SOUNDS
OF DARKNESS

Jago Moon sat silently in the gloom.

He rummaged in his satchel and found a half-smoked cigar, which he chewed for a moment and then lit, inhaling slowly. The leather chair he was sitting in was comfortable and he eased himself back into its embrace. That felt so good that he lifted his booted feet and rested them on the desk in front of him. All that was missing, he thought, was a coal fire and a glass of brandy.

Moon was pleased that he could not see his surroundings. He could imagine what sort of decor Claw Carter would choose for his private sanctum. The professor masqueraded before the world as a man of history and learning, but Moon knew what his real interest was.

Death.

He had prayed long and hard before going against Mother Shepherd's wishes. Maybe it was because he was so stubborn himself, but he simply couldn't imagine Benjamin Kingdom leaving the Legion and joining the Watchers just because Nathaniel and the Weeping Man asked him nicely. Moon had been so bullheaded in his own youth that whatever he had been asked to do, he had always done the exact opposite, and Ben had a lot of that in him too. That was why he had come up with another plan. A more direct route to the same destination, he hoped.

When he left the eyrie he hadn't told anyone where he was going or why; this was his responsibility and his alone. After some fiddling with a set of skeleton keys and a jemmy, he had made his way into the echoing halls of the British Museum. The nightwatchmen were all dim-witted fellows apparently, and they had no idea that they were entertaining guests that night.

Moon had made it his business to familiarize himself with the whole of London: the back lanes and the thoroughfares, the East End and the West. He had tap-tap-tapped his way around all the great public buildings, measuring their spaces by echoes and scents, just in case the day came when the knowledge would be valuable to the Watcher cause. So, feeling his way around the museum earlier, he had quickly found the corridor he was searching for. His hands recognized the length of knotted braid which forbade entry to visitors, and he'd carefully lifted one end from its brass hook and slipped into the private section. Carter's room was in the basement and there was only one set of stairs leading down. Once in that corridor, the correct door was easy enough to find, his nimble fingers reading the names etched into the brass doorplates.

Professor James Carter. It sounded so respectable!

Safely inside, he'd made his way to the desk and sat himself down. He hummed a little tune to himself while he waited for one of the most evil men in Britain to come pay him a visit.

He didn't have to wait long before his wish was granted.

The door swished open, and he felt the change in the air as a man slipped into the room. Although Carter probably thought that he was moving quietly, Moon followed his every step; the soft squeaks of the leather trench coat, the measured shallow breaths, the slow deliberate way he placed his feet.

Carter was in front of him.

Beside him.

Behind him.

Moon braced himself for what was to come.

"What have we here?" growled Carter, his claw pressing against the flesh of Moon's throat. "A Watcher spy?"

Jago Moon laughed. Everything was going according to plan.

When Moon came to, he was being dragged down a tunnel, his head throbbing where Carter had coshed him. Admittedly, that *wasn't* part of the plan. However, when he reached out with his ears, the sounds that came back to him made him smile. Not that they were pleasant noises to listen to; on the contrary, they were the very sounds of darkness. Moon smiled because he had succeeded where no Watcher had before: he was being taken right into the heart of the Under.

His nostrils tasted the air, rank with bodies and smoke; the grease of sweat, the meaty taint of the slaughterhouse. There were so many voices, echoing around him, pounding inside his skull. Low conversations, heavy with menace. Whispers of evil. Somewhere, a child was sobbing. He heard shouting, swearing, screaming. And other sounds that did not belong on this earth and chilled him to his soul.

He had exaggerated his achievement, he knew that. Pride was one of the many failings that he confessed when he was on his knees in prayer. Watchers *had* been into the Under before, but previously not one of them had come out again. That was why Moon had been so keen to undertake this mission on his own; any fool could get himself captured, the real skill was in escaping afterwards.

He liked to think that he knew a bit about Benjamin Kingdom. After all, how many conversations had they had down the years, sitting in that smoky corner in the Jolly Tar, talking foolishly about books? There *was* something special about the boy, he could see that, looking back; submerged beneath Ben's quick mouth and even quicker fingers, there had always been potential. What Moon hadn't perceived was that this cheeky mudlark would one day hold the balance between the forces of light and dark.

The Uncreated One definitely has a sense of humour, he thought.

In many ways Moon was proud of Ben, although he would never say it to his face. The boy worked hard and never complained about his lot. He found things to enjoy in a life that was full of hardships. He had a spirit of adventure which survived all the knocks along the way.

Perhaps that was what was needed in the Hand of Heaven. A hope that endures; the courage to believe that life can be better.

Shame about that cocky mouth, though.

A sharp jab in the ribs brought Moon back to the present.

"You can walk on your own now, granddad. I'm sick of doing all the work for you," snarled his escort, taking his supporting arm from around Moon's shoulders. "But try anything funny and I'll gut you right here."

Moon didn't doubt it. The man who had been bundling him along was over six feet tall, judging by the direction of the voice, and built like a brick privy, based on the heaviness of his foot. He was wearing a thick apron which brushed against his thighs as he walked and smelled very strongly of fish. That, combined with his accent which put him somewhere between Eastcheap and Cannon Street, all confirmed that he worked at Billingsgate Fish Market. *If anyone could gut me*, Moon thought grimly, *this man certainly could.*

The fishmonger underestimated him though, and that was a big mistake. No one ever saw a blind man as a threat. Moon chuckled. He hadn't been bound and gagged. The poor man hadn't even confiscated his walking cane.

So it was that once he had fully regained consciousness

Moon calmly walked himself into prison, tap-tap-tapping his way through the Under. Listening to the flow of the corridors; hearing his way to escape. Although it had always been a reckless plan, he was beginning to think that it might actually work.

It only relied on Ben to do the one thing he was really good at: open his mouth and get himself into trouble. Surely Benjamin Kingdom could manage that!

At the prison door, Jago Moon froze.

The stench that waited for him on the other side was the foulest thing he had ever breathed. The excrement didn't bother him; everyone who lived near the Thames was used to that smell. Nor was it the waft of rotting meat and damp straw that came out to greet him. Jago Moon halted because the room stank of despair.

The fishmonger placed his broad hand in the middle of Moon's back and propelled him through. "Enjoy your stay," he jeered, as Moon stumbled and fell to the floor. Behind him, Moon could hear the sound of a key turning and the fishmonger's harsh laughter.

The cell had been home to so many prisoners in its time, it was as if their fear had seeped into the brickwork. Suddenly Moon felt alone and very afraid.

Please don't leave me in here alone for too long, Ben, he prayed.

CHAPTER 32

SANCTUARY

Although Ben's head was pounding when he regained consciousness, he was glad that Mickelwhite had stepped in to stop him when he did. He didn't understand what had come over him on the rooftop and felt ashamed of what he had done; even though Bedlam had started it.

Ben had no idea how long he had blacked out for, but he knew that it must have been most of the day. He had never felt more tired and drained. It wasn't just the result of his physical exertions either. Ben recognized that something unnatural was taking an appalling toll on his mind and spirit. Something small and round and silver. It was as if he had acquired a leech that was slowly and steadily sucking the life from him, leaving a shell that looked like Ben but was completely hollow on the inside.

As he opened one eye it took him a second to recognize that he was back in the Under again, and that they were all there to "greet" him: Captain Mickelwhite; twitchy Jimmy Dips; Alexander Valentine, looking more sickly than before; Hans Schulman, with his square Germanic shoulders; poor crippled Munro; and, last in line, a puffy-faced John Bedlam. Ruby Johnson was there too, standing behind the others, her eyes fixed firmly on the floor.

Not one of them looked pleased to see him, Ben thought.

That also probably explained why they were all standing up and he was bound at the wrists and lying on the floor.

While the boys glared at him, Ben noticed that Ruby was steadfastly avoiding catching his eye. She looked uncomfortable and obviously felt ashamed, and Ben was pleased; that was the way that traitors *should* feel. And yet, there was still a part of him that would have found a crumb of comfort in her emerald gaze.

Ben curled up in agony as a really juicy kick in the belly helped him to come completely to his senses. He looked up to see John Bedlam on the end of that boot, grinning wickedly through fat lips and a black eye.

"You kick a bit like a girl, too," Ben quipped. *Same-old, same-old*, he thought: laughing on the outside, hurting on the inside. He tensed his stomach muscles, ready for a second visit from Bedlam's boot.

But for the second time it was Mickelwhite who was his saviour. "Leave it, John," he said. "We have been summoned to the sanctuary to give an account of last night's little excursion." He made a small sound then to prove that this was his idea of a really witty comment. "I will be very interested to see how our new associate talks his way out of this one."

So will I, thought Ben, as they led him away.

They came to a halt outside a pair of massive bronze doors. They towered above Ben, four times as tall as he was. Like the door of the armoury, they were covered with images of angels and winged beasts with the heads of birds and lions and bulls. Ben looked closer and then recoiled. These angels were savage. They fought with teeth and claws and swords and spears, and other weapons that he couldn't name, but which would be just as effective at cutting out your heart. They were not at all like the fat-faced cherubs he had seen at Cowpat Cowper's Sunday school.

Nor were they like the noble angel who flew with the Watchers.

"When we are inside the sanctuary, nobody speak without my say-so," said Mickelwhite curtly as he led the way.

For the first time ever, Ben felt like doing exactly as he was told. And yet...

"Blow me down," he said as he stepped inside. He really did want to hold his tongue but he just couldn't help himself. The sanctuary of the Legion was an architectural miracle. Every Londoner was so in awe of the work of Sir Christopher Wren and the dome of St Paul's. *If only they could see the work of Alasdair Valentine*, thought Ben.

The craftsmen of the Legion had laboured underground to build a cathedral of their own; equal, but opposite. It was filled with a thousand candles: on the floor, in niches, in the walls, on pillars, in sconces. And yet they couldn't create enough light to fill the inky shadows that encircled them. There was movement in those pools of darkness, Ben realized; shapes that were not quite human, whispers and spiteful laughter.

Everywhere that Ben laid his eyes, he found something to be afraid of. The columns that he had seen in the Egyptian's workshop were dwarfed by the ones here.

Each massive pillar took the form of a man or woman with the head of a beast, their faces evil and cruel, their arms arching forward to support the vaulted roof. And as their hideous splendour drew his eyes up to the domed ceiling, Ben was chilled to the marrow by what he discovered there.

There were…creatures… What else could he call them? Horrible things, that roosted in the eaves, holding tight to the stonework with strange elongated hands and feet, and nails like talons. Their bodies might once have been human, but their heads and wings belonged to a nightmare.

The bird-men, Ben realized with a gasp. No wonder poor Mr. Smutts had been scared half to death.

Mickelwhite brought them to a halt in front of a vast golden throne and then kneeled before it, his head bowed. Ben followed suit, but not before he had taken a good look at who he was bowing to.

Claw Carter sat upon the throne.

Ben knew then that he had been terribly wrong to compare this man to his father. Jonas Kingdom was decent and honest and down to earth. Not full of selfish ambition and vanity like the man seated before him.

How could I ever have wanted to be like Claw Carter? he wondered.

Although his hands were still tied behind his back, Ben

could feel the ache of the Legion mark. He wished that he could scrub it off. Perhaps he could put his hand into a fire and burn it away?

He thought of the Coin in his pocket and wanted to be rid of that too.

"I have been informed of your failure," Claw Carter intoned in a sonorous voice. "I am...disappointed." Ben guessed that something far worse than a dressing-down was coming their way. "You all know the Legion law..." Ben didn't, but he couldn't put his hand up to ask. "You must decide amongst yourselves," Carter continued. "You must choose which one of you shall carry the punishment, or all face the wrath of the Feathered Men."

Carter observed them with a sardonic smile: Ruby Johnson buttoned down tight, while the Legion boys shuffled anxiously.

And Benjamin Kingdom, looking on with absolute contempt.

The more chance Carter had to study Ben, the more he could see the possibility that he could be the Hand of Hell. He was an angry boy, strong willed, defiant. Those were all great qualities in a general of the Legion. Provided, of course, that he could be trained to do as he was told. What was the point in having a fighting dog, if it didn't come to heel when its master snapped his fingers?

If Ben Kingdom could be made to obey him, then Carter would definitely be able to make a place for him in his future plans. And fortunately, two more bargaining chips had fallen into his lap that night. Both were languishing in the cells. Both were men that were dear to Ben Kingdom.

Carter wondered how much pressure he would have to put on his captives before Ben capitulated. Was the boy so pig-headed that one of them would have to die first? One of them knew where the Coin was, that was certain. Just as it was certain that they would hand it over to him in the end, *beg* him to take it from them. Every man had his breaking point.

In the depths of the dark cathedral of the Legion, at the far end of the long nave, was what Carter considered to be its greatest wonder: the steeple. On the surface, a steeple always stretched upwards, a finger pointing the way to Heaven. Here in the Under, it stretched down towards the centre of the earth. A huge black pit, that even the candlelight could not penetrate, descending through solid rock. Rumours said that there were beings that lived at the bottom that had never seen daylight at all.

What would it take to break Ben Kingdom? thought

Carter. Would it be sufficient to dangle him over the edge? Or would he have to be thrown in and left in the darkness for a while?

There was only one way to find out.

Ben said nothing in his own defence. Mickelwhite and Bedlam could hardly wait to point the finger at him and the others fell quickly into line. All except for Ruby, who folded her arms and refused to take part. Instead, Ben took the opportunity to wriggle his wrists free while they were busy settling his fate, letting the rope drop silently to the floor.

The more time he spent with the Legion, the more he recognized that these people were not his friends. He was more alone here than he had ever been in Old Gravel Lane.

His mother's Bible was still in his pocket and his right hand reached for it then. His heart always ached for her at Christmas. He had known her for one day, and he had missed her every day since. He missed Nathaniel as well, he realized. Looking back, they should never have allowed imaginary walls to be built between them; grief should have brought them together, not pushed them apart.

Ben thought of his father too. His dear, beloved pa.

Stuff the Legion, stuff the Coin! What was he hanging around here for? He had a family to rescue.

"Come on then!" Ben shouted. "You've picked me, so let's get on with it!"

Overhead, one of the Feathered Men shrieked and Ben felt a shiver run the length of his spine as the creature detached itself from its resting place and took to the air. It dived down, its taloned feet reaching out towards him, like a kestrel seizing a hare. The creature screeched as it descended and Ben could see its thin yellow tongue inside the black maw of its mouth.

A moment of panic flooded Ben's chest and he realized that he hadn't returned the Coin to its hiding place in his hat. Could the Feathered Man smell it on him? he wondered. Did he stink of Roman silver?

Thinking on his feet, Ben thrust his hand into his pocket and whipped out the battered Bible, holding it out in front of him like a shield. In the stories that he loved, vampires were repelled by garlic and werewolves by the touch of silver; perhaps this might have the same effect on these nightmare creatures? Ben fancied that he saw fear in its cold avian eyes and it shrieked all the louder as it recognized the holy book. The Feathered Man pulled out of its dive at the last instant, but not before it had ripped the Bible from Ben's fingers and scattered its pages across the floor.

So this is it then, thought Ben. Whichever way he counted them, the odds of getting out alive were just too great. He was trapped beneath the ground, surrounded on all sides. Alone and unarmed.

Mickelwhite was laughing. The Feathered Men were screaming.

Claw Carter was clapping, his hand slapping against his claw in great amusement. "Bravo!" he said. "I like a boy with spirit."

"Oh really?" said Ben, Carter's arrogance proving the spur he needed to keep on fighting. "Well you'll *love* this then."

Looking round for inspiration, Ben grabbed one of the metal sconces, ripping off the fat candle to reveal the sharp iron spike beneath. Then, holding it in two hands like a spear, he began to edge his way towards the door.

Carter continued to applaud.

Schulman made a lunge for Ben but only succeeded in colliding with Mickelwhite, sending them both sprawling when Ben jabbed with his makeshift weapon. Valentine tried to work his way behind Ben but, swinging the heavy sconce like a club, Ben brought him down.

Carter snapped his fingers then and made an ugly rasping sound, which the Feathered Men clearly understood to be an order. Ben watched as they responded.

Three more Feathered Men dropped down from the roof and began to circle him in the air, like vultures waiting for the moment to fall on their prey. Meanwhile, Bedlam began to close in, grinning manically. Ben spun, managing to keep him out of arm's reach with the sconce, but he was getting tired and they all knew it.

Without warning, one of the Feathered Men swooped down and grabbed hold of Ben's weapon with its clawed feet and then, with a single beat of its wings, yanked it out of his grasp, leaving him defenceless. The other two foul creatures didn't waste their opportunity, diving down and knocking him to the ground, their talons piercing Ben's flesh as they half-carried, half-dragged him back before the throne.

One of the Feathered Men hopped onto Ben's chest, punching all the air from his lungs, and pinning his arms to the ground. It studied Ben with its huge eyes; unblinking, unfeeling. It opened its beak and rasped a shrill cry in Ben's face. It was like looking into the face of a nightmare, thought Ben. Everything that was dark and evil had come to visit him.

The sanctuary fell silent.

"Where were we?" said Carter with fake forgetfulness. "Oh yes, I remember. You have chosen the victim to pay the price for your failure."

The Feathered Men handed Ben over to Bedlam and Mickelwhite, and they bundled him across the stone floor until he was standing on the edge of a precipice. Although Ben resisted and dug in his heels every inch of the way, there wasn't much he could do against their kicks and shoves. Bedlam pressed his bruised and swollen face against Ben's and rasped in his ear: "Got anything clever to say this time, mate?"

Ben's feet dangled half on and half off the lip of a hole so deep that no light could reach the bottom. The slightest push from behind would send him tumbling. Above his head, the Feathered Men squawked their approval, their shrieks as sharp as a razor's edge. Ben was right out of witty comebacks.

Carter could see the fear in Ben's eyes as he gazed into the pit. It was a delicious moment, and Carter savoured it. If Ben Kingdom *was* to become the Left Hand, then his rebirth was destined to be a painful one; the ancient texts were clear on this. Betrayal, suffering and torment would all be required if Ben was to be stripped of every last shred of goodness that might remain within him. The Left Hand would be a creature governed by hate, bitterness, and spite. This young man, who rolled with the punches and came back smiling, would have to be put to death, and replaced by a new Benjamin Kingdom, who looked at the world with resentment, not excitement.

Carter allowed his own eyes to explore the depths of the pit and he shuddered. There was no question that Ben would come out a different man.

Carter glanced at his pocket watch. "It is now almost eleven," he declared. "We shall meet again at midnight and make good this act of contrition by casting your sacrificial offering into the pit."

That would be me then, thought Ben soberly.

He gazed down into the endless black until he began to feel dizzy. Was it his imagination or could he hear scurrying and whispering in the depths?

Apparently, when the clock struck twelve he would be finding out.

CHAPTER 33

CHOSEN TO DIE

After Carter had issued his decree, Ben was marched away. Although he had just hours to live, he was grateful nevertheless to get out of that hateful place.

Naturally it was Mickelwhite and Bedlam who were given the task of taking Ben to the cell where he would wait until it was his allotted time to die. The other members of the brigade had all seemed as relieved as he was to get out of the sanctuary and had slunk away into the Under as soon as they got the chance. Ruby Johnson included, Ben noted.

So this was it then, Ben realized coldly as he arrived at the dungeon door. *Ladies and gentlemen, Ben Kingdom stands before you under sentence of death.*

"Hope you like your new accommodation," said Bedlam, opening the stout wooden door and propelling Ben inside with a shove that sent him falling face down on the floor. With his hands tied behind his back again, Ben had no way of saving himself and he landed heavily, his face slapping against the flagstones, his mouth tasting rotting straw and stale urine.

Ben wanted to say something to prove that they hadn't beaten him, but his mouth was full of blood and his heart was full of fear. In the end, he managed to scramble up onto his knees and spit at Bedlam's feet, forcing out a hollow laugh.

Bedlam reacted in a flash but Mickelwhite was quick to restrain him and hold him, snarling, in the doorway.

"Patience," urged Mickelwhite. "Let's see if he's still laughing when we throw him in the pit."

I wouldn't count on it, thought Ben as the cell door slammed shut and the heavy key turned in the lock. He listened to their footsteps receding into the distance.

The only light in the cell came through the grilled window in the door, but the rattle of claws on stone told him that he was not alone. His flesh crawled. *Rats.*

He watched a filthy rodent as it scuttled out of the shadows and made its way towards him. Ben backed away. "Get out of it," he hissed, kicking straw in the rat's direction but to no avail. He knew it was irrational – it was only a rat after all – and yet with each twitch of its whiskers, each jerk of its pink naked tail, each flash of its long yellow incisors, Ben could feel his calm being gnawed away.

Then a sudden movement from the inky black at the far end of the cell caught Ben's attention and he turned to see a missile whistling through the air. The stone struck the rat hard enough to make it yelp and then scuttle quickly for the safety of its bolt-hole.

"Good shot," said Ben. Then, his back wet with nervous sweat, he searched for his rescuer in the gloom.

"Come here, boy," said a familiar voice from the darkest corner of the cell. "Let me get those ropes off you."

"Mr. Moon!" said Ben, delighted. "I didn't see you there."

"Welcome to my world," said Jago Moon. Ben wasn't entirely sure whether he was joking.

Gratefully Ben turned his back and let the blind man set him free. "Thank you," he said quietly, and he rubbed his wrists where the ropes had chaffed his skin raw. Overwhelmed with questions, he slumped down on the straw beside Moon, not sure where to start. "So you're a prisoner too then?"

"Aye, lad."

"So does that mean that you're one of the other lot, a Watcher?"

"Aye, lad."

"And you've known about the Legion all along?"

Moon nodded.

"And you never thought to tell me about any of this?" Ben sounded indignant.

"You were a silly boy, always lost in your books."

"Books that *you* sold me!"

"Always dreaming," Moon continued. "Always answering back. Never listening."

"Well, I'm listening now," said Ben petulantly.

"Good," said Moon, "because if we are both about to be executed, there isn't time for me to repeat myself, so pin back your lugholes and keep that mouth of yours shut."

"How can you be so calm about all this?" Ben was exasperated.

"Because I understand and you don't, Benjamin Kingdom," Moon barked. "Now pay attention and listen to me!" His tone brooked no discussion. "I don't know what lies Carter has already filled your head with, but you need to know about the Watchers if you are going to start making some better decisions."

"The Watchers are spies, ruled over by a hag," said Ben. "Or that's what I was told, anyway."

286

Moon sighed. "The Watchers are like lighthouse keepers. We warn of dangers, we shine a light in the darkness, we keep a constant vigil for those in peril of being drowned or washed away. We guide the shipwrecked to the safety of the shore. We save the lost." Moon sighed. "There is terrible evil in the world, Ben, and though the history books don't say so, through the generations there have always been Watchers who have fought to keep that evil in check."

"So if the Watchers are like a lighthouse, who are the Legion then. Pirates?"

"No. The Legion are the waves, tearing away at the foundation stones of society, day by day and drip by drip. They sweep up the unwary and the unwise, dragging them down into the slime and filth in the darkest depths. They are the black tide, as unrelenting and without mercy as the cruellest sea. And if you dare to stand against them, they will dash you to pieces upon the rocks."

It was beginning to sound to Ben as if taking the Mark hadn't been his best decision. "But where do I fit into all this?" he asked. "Why is an angel with a sword looking for me?"

"Because you have been chosen, Benjamin Kingdom."

"Chosen? No more riddles, please," Ben demanded. "Chosen for what?"

"Chosen to die," Moon said matter-of-factly, as if he were discussing the price of eggs.

"Tell me something I don't know," Ben snapped. "I can even tell you what time I'm gonna snuff it, if you like!"

"What did I say about listening?" Jago Moon paused, until he was sure that Ben was concentrating again. "The sacred prophecies of the Watchers tell of a young man who will become a great leader, called the Hand, and will guide his people to victory. Just as you can decide what to do with your own two hands – whether to use them to hurt or to heal, to give or to take – so the boy must decide which side he will fight for: Watcher or Legion, good or evil. He must choose for himself whether to be the great and powerful Right Hand of Heaven, or the wicked and spiteful Left Hand of Hell."

"And then die," Ben added glibly, trying to distract himself from his inner turmoil. It was so much to take in. This great leader couldn't really be him, could it? How could he be expected to lead an army when he only made it through each week with bluff and bravado? And then his right hand began to throb in answer to his own question. *The Hand*. He really *was* different to the other boys on Old Gravel Lane, after all.

"Yes, and then die," Moon replied. "But not as you understand it. The Hand of Heaven *will* die. He will die to himself, set aside all his own worldly ambition, and live for others. If you choose to follow the Watchers, then that is the future you face, Benjamin Kingdom."

"Well, why didn't you say so before?" said Ben, rising to his feet.

In the cell next door, Jonas Kingdom drifted in and out of consciousness.

He was more tired than he had ever been in his life. He had forced himself to go without sleep for several days. How could he rest when he hadn't found Ben?

The places he had been... Through the rookeries, all around the deadly Tiger Bay district, peering into the frightening places of the city. He didn't have a photograph to show people what his lost boy looked like – they had never had that sort of money – but he could describe him vividly. Ben was the absolute spit of the amazing woman who had carried him, right down to the fiery red hair and the lopsided smile. Eventually he came across someone who claimed to have seen him, a Chinese man who told him that a boy fitting that description had visited his laundry a few nights before.

And it was when Jonas stepped outside that laundry that the Feathered Men had attacked him. It was almost as if they had been waiting there to capture him and drag him away to this dungeon. But he hadn't gone with them easily. That was why his body was so battered and bruised. Tentatively, he put his hand to his face, exploring the lumps and swellings around his eyes and across his jaw. He turned over on the straw, trying to find a way to rest his body that didn't cause him pain. Then he shut his eyes.

He was probably dreaming, because he thought that he could hear his son's voice drifting though the wall.

"Ben..." His lips made the shape of the name but no sound came out. *I'll find you.*

"So how come you're sat here, twiddling your thumbs?" Ben asked Jago Moon.

"Because, young Benjamin," Moon explained wearily, "the Uncreated One told me to wait here for you."

"So you get messages from a higher power, is that what you are trying to tell me?" Ben wasn't sure about any of this. "Nice trick if you can do it."

"And *you* can do it," Moon replied. "That is just one of the many skills that it will be my onerous duty to teach you...if the Uncreated One can grant me sufficient patience."

Mollified by the warmth that lay just beneath the surface of Moon's words, Ben went to his old friend's side.

"Here, we can use these," said Moon, reaching into his jacket pocket.

"Two fountain pens? Very helpful."

"They *look* like fountain pens," Moon snapped. "But each one is packed full of gunpowder."

Ben's eyes lit up.

"All you need do is extract the fuse like this..." Moon continued, twisting the pen and pulling out a short length of wire. "Light it like this, then shove it into the keyhole... and Bob's your uncle! We'll be out of here in no time."

"And what happens after we've blown the door?" Ben asked, while the pair of them took cover.

"Oh," said Jago Moon, his heavy brows drawn into a frown. "The Uncreated One has just told me that you are in charge after that."

CHAPTER 34

UNDER THE THAMES

When Ruby heard the distant rumble of the explosion, she knew that somehow it had to be Ben Kingdom and she smiled. She had loitered as near to the cells as she dared without drawing attention to herself, although she hadn't decided if she was going to help Ben break out or just try to see him one more time through the bars. Whatever she did, she had to try to explain what happened, to tell him that she was just obeying Carter's orders, to say that she was sorry at least. Her heart began to beat rapidly as she headed in the direction of the blast, and she wasn't sure whether it was due to shock or some other, more dangerous, emotion.

Ruby Johnson was not used to feeling this way. Uncertain. Confused. She wanted her world to be black and white again. She had worked so hard to develop her public persona: Ruby Johnson, so confident! Ruby Johnson, so self-assured! Except that she wasn't, not really; not on the inside where it mattered. And it was all Ben Kingdom's fault.

As discreetly as she could, Ruby set off in the direction of the bomb blast. Others would come running soon, she knew that, but she wanted to get there first.

A thought struck her as she ran. It surprised her at first, but the more she rolled it around in her mind, the more right it felt.

If Ben was escaping from the Under, he might want some company. Perhaps she could leave the Legion after all.

Emerging from the matchwood that used to be a door, Ben linked Moon's arm through his, and began to pick his way through the maze of underground corridors.

Ben knew that he didn't have the luxury of being able to deliberate on his choices, he would just have to go with his gut. "If you are going to start talking to me, Uncreated One, this would be a really good time!" he breathed. He dragged Moon onwards, trying to put as much distance between them and the cell as he could.

"Quickly, Benjamin," warned Jago Moon. "I can hear footsteps."

"Well, bully for you," said Ben, feeling the pressure.

Ben hesitated at the junction of two tunnels, one well-lit, the other filled with shadows. Less candles equals less use, Ben reasoned, and chose the dark path.

It felt like the right decision at first.

But as they plunged headlong from one pool of light to another, he started to worry. They were definitely heading away from the busy communal areas at the hub of the Under, but Ben had no way of knowing whether that was good or bad.

When they reached the last of the torches, Ben took one off the wall and brandished it ahead of him. For some time the passage had been sloping steadily downwards, but the only direction that Ben really wanted to be taking them was up and out into the light. No other tunnels led off this one either apparently, not to the left or the right, and so they had no choice except to keep going onwards. It was growing colder too, Ben noticed, and twice he felt cold water drip down on him from the roof. These were not good signs. Ben had the sinking feeling that this was going to turn out to be a dead end, with the emphasis on *dead*.

"We have to turn back," Ben decided.

"It's too late," said Moon sadly, shaking his head. "The Legion are on our heels."

"How many?"

"Only three by the sound of it – one of them is more stealthy than the others, probably a girl."

"Three?" said Ben. "We can handle them."

"I don't doubt it," said Moon, "but I'm not sure how we'd fare against their companion."

Then Ben heard it too, echoing down the tunnel: the hideous shrieking of a Feathered Man.

Was it really that simple? Ruby wondered.

If Ben could walk away from this life, why shouldn't she?

She passed the cell door, which was hanging off its hinges, a ragged hole where the lock had once been, and it made a smile break out on her face.

"What a team we could make, Ben Kingdom," she said appreciatively.

She picked up her step.

There weren't many tunnels that Ben could have taken from here and she had a hunch that Ben would have headed straight for the wrong one.

The boy needs me, she thought happily.

The water was dripping more heavily from the roof now.

It hissed as it rained on the torch and Ben prayed that they wouldn't be trapped down here in the dark. The tunnel continued to slope downwards and the walls had become oily with slime and running water, making Ben grimace each time his fingers connected with the slick stonework, as cold and repellent as rotting flesh.

Ben's feet were sodden. Brackish water had seeped through his boots and with each step the water was getting higher. It was at his ankles already and the tunnel still showed no sign of curving upwards and out.

"We must be under the Thames," said Moon, holding fast to Ben's arm as they did their best to negotiate the slippery stones.

"That at least explains the smell," said Ben, wrinkling his nose against the stench of filth and decay.

"We need to hurry, Benjamin," Moon urged. "Our pursuers are getting nearer."

"I'm amazed we've had such an easy run of it so far," Ben confessed. It was surely just a matter of time before the Legion caught up with them, he knew. His only hope was that they could make it to the surface in time to have it away on their toes.

Moon squeezed Ben's arm so fiercely then that it made Ben wince.

"What was that for?"

"Brave heart, Benjamin, I can hear footsteps ahead of us too."

"How many?" asked Ben.

"It sounds like hundreds," Moon replied.

CHAPTER 35

OUT OF THE BLACK

A sonorous bell rang through the Under.

Ruby knew what it meant. It was the call to arms. Someone else must have discovered Ben's escape. Ruby could hear the pounding of running feet, orders being shouted, somewhere a baby screaming. The Feathered Men had been roused too, she realized with a shudder, their piercing shrieks adding to the pandemonium.

Ruby Johnson ran on. She was running out of time.

So the boy had escaped.

Why am I not surprised? thought Carter.

After all, if Ben Kingdom really was the Left Hand, the Son of the Sinister, then he would have guile and cunning aplenty. That was why he had deliberately pushed the boy into a corner, to test his mettle; to see how he would react. If Ben gave in to anger and hatred, then all well and good; the sooner he could fulfil his destiny at the dark heart of the Legion.

If, however, Ben was overcome by weaker emotions instead, then he was sure to go running to the Watchers. Such feeble qualities as mercy and forgiveness and love would be welcomed there, Carter scoffed.

And this was where the true brilliance of his scheme lay, Carter congratulated himself. It was not by chance that Ben had been placed in a cell with that reprobate Watcher, Jago Moon. Carter knew that if Ben did try to break out, then Moon would be only too happy to take the boy straight to the Watchers' lair. All that Carter need do was let the pair of them run, and allow them to lead him straight to wherever the Watchers had pitched camp that night.

He would follow at a distance, and then unleash the Feathered Men.

The Watchers were bound to be keeping the Coin somewhere in their eyrie. No doubt that grasping hag, Mother Shepherd, would be clutching it tight to her withered bosom. He would tear their encampment apart to find it, and tear out her heart for good measure.

Tonight was win-win for Claw Carter.

The Christmas presents just kept on coming. And he hadn't even been a good boy.

Ruby knew that the light around the bend in the tunnel had to belong to Ben.

She could hear two sets of feet sloshing about in the water and so she had assumed that Ben had felt obliged to take the disgusting old blind man along with him. That wasn't important for the moment; they could always ditch him later, Ruby decided.

She was taking it nice and carefully, relying on the light from Ben's torch in the distance. The floor of the tunnel had been made treacherous by the muck of the River Thames and the water was already up to her thighs. Each well-placed step she took narrowed the distance between her and Ben and she was beginning to feel rather pleased with herself again.

Then she heard a sound which stole all her confidence away.

A dreadful squawking noise, shrill and angry, filled the tunnel behind her with its wrath.

※

Mickelwhite had known that Ben would make a move, and so he and Bedlam had been waiting for it. They had a few old scores to settle with Ben Kingdom, and just to ensure they proved their point, they had brought a friend with them.

It was amazing what sort of loyalty you could buy for a leg of mutton, Mickelwhite thought.

"They're coming," said Ben. He could see the flicker of another torch approaching from the gloom behind them and hear other feet wading through the water accompanied by the terrible screaming of the Feathered Men.

"They're coming," said Jago Moon, his blind eyes staring into the tunnel ahead of them.

It was then that Ben finally heard what Moon had been hearing all along; the insane song of a horde of rats swimming towards them out of the black.

A Feathered Man was pouncing along the tunnel towards Ruby, bounding from wall to ceiling and back again, finding purchase on the stonework with its talons. Ruby could see its beak snapping, the thin yellow tongue protruding, desperate for the taste of flesh. The creature had a metal collar around its neck, attached to a long length of chain. And on the end of that chain was Captain Mickelwhite, the Feathered Man dragging him forward with each lurch, like a bloodhound on the scent.

Blundering through the water beside Mickelwhite, a flaming torch in his hand and a nasty smile on his face, was John Bedlam. Ruby's heart sank.

"On the hunt too, eh?" Mickelwhite said. He seemed delighted to meet her. The feeling was not mutual.

"Look!" shouted Bedlam, pointing wildly. "He's there!"

Mickelwhite let the chain slip through his fingers and the Feathered Man leaped free.

"Kingdom will rue the day he betrayed the Legion," said Mickelwhite with a spiteful leer.

Ben was trapped.

Behind them, one of the Feathered Men was crawling along the roof of the tunnel, its round eyes filled with hate, its beak clacking. Mickelwhite was there too, with his pet bully-boy, John Bedlam. Ben could see them as they turned a corner in the tunnel and came into view: two assassins in the torchlight.

Ahead of them, the water was writhing with rats. Fat

body upon fat body. A sea of vermin rushing their way.

For all that – the terror, the horror, the promise of a painful death – only one thing hurt him: the girl who had led Mickelwhite straight to him.

"Ruby!" He shouted her name with such force that flecks of hot spittle came out with it. "I hate you!"

He could see her skulking behind Bedlam; there was no light in her eyes. "I thought you were my friend," he added, but not loud enough for anyone except Jago Moon to hear.

At that moment, the first of the rats found him in the waist-deep water, and began to clamber up his torso, punching small holes in his shirt and chest as it scrabbled for a grip. More rats climbed out of the water onto his arms, his back, his hat; it was as if they had been shipwrecked and he was an island. Every part of Ben's brain was in revolt; he would have screamed except he was afraid that a rat would take refuge in the cave of his mouth.

Ben thrust the torch into the mass of rats, not caring if he burned himself in the process. The stench of scorching fur met his nostrils, but it was hopeless: for every rat that fell away, two more took its place. The Feathered Man would be upon him in seconds too; the black plumage of its head loomed at him like an executioner's cowl.

So much for the promise of power, thought Ben.

Then a desperate idea struck him and while he continued to fend off the rats with his flailing torch, Ben reached inside into his pocket with his free hand.

"Don't do it, boy," said Moon, when he heard the rasp of the fuse being lit and realized what Ben was planning. "You'll bring the roof down on us!"

"Too late," said Ben as he jabbed the second pen-bomb into the soft mortar between the bricks in the tunnel wall.

Perhaps it was his proximity to death, but a strange urge took over Ben at that moment and he reached into his pocket to draw out the Coin that had been slumbering there. He held it aloft between his finger and thumb and twisted it so that it caught the torchlight. Even the Feathered Man halted, recognizing the significance of the small piece of silver.

"I'm joining the Watchers," Ben shouted, "and I'm taking your precious Coin with me!"

Moon stepped in then and took control. He grabbed hold of Ben with surprising strength, manhandling him up the tunnel and out of the immediate line of the explosive that was about to go off in his face.

"For the Hand of Heaven," said Moon with despair, "you ain't too bright, are you?"

Ben didn't have time to respond, because at that instant

Moon shifted his weight and threw them both down beneath the surface of the water, while above them the tunnel blossomed with flame.

DAY SIX
25TH DECEMBER –
CHRISTMAS DAY, 1891

CHAPTER 36

THE RIGHT CHOICE

Jago Moon held Ben beneath the water while the world turned white. Eventually they both broke the surface, coughing and gasping, their heads emerging through a bobbing layer of rat corpses.

In the last flickering flames of the explosion, Ben surveyed the scene. The blast hadn't been enough to bring the River Thames flooding down on their heads, thank goodness. The thick London clay continued to hold back the waters, but for how much longer he couldn't be sure. However, a huge chunk of the tunnel wall had collapsed, blocking the passage completely, with the Feathered Man and the Legion trapped on one side, and Ben and Moon on the other.

There wasn't time to think about who the blast might have killed.

Ben could hear someone or something clawing against the rubble on the far side, so he knew that not everyone was dead. Had Ruby escaped? *Did he care?*

With a hiss, the flame of Ben's torch gave up the ghost and the darkness around them became absolute.

"Come on," he said to Moon affectionately. "Take me home." He picked up his battered hat and, even though it was dripping wet shoved it on his head. Then he let the blind man lead him along the tunnel, the scraping of talons on stone echoing in their minds.

Sniffing and listening all the way, Moon eventually brought them to the foot of a rusted ladder. With every step, he longed to tell Ben about the Coin that he was carrying but he remembered Mother Shepherd's warning. She felt that the safest course of action was to allow Ben to be blissfully ignorant. She was afraid that Ben would do something rash if he knew what the Coin really was. Moon raised an eyebrow; she wasn't wrong on that score, and besides, he reasoned, they would soon be back amongst the Watchers and Josiah could take possession of the damned thing and destroy it once and for all.

"I smell clean air," he said.

Ben went first and heaved open a trapdoor. He had never been more delighted to breathe in the stink of the Thames. *Cleanish air, anyway*, thought Ben.

It was the early hours of Christmas morning and the sky above was the indigo blue of ink on water. It took Ben a couple of seconds to gain his bearings. They were on the south side of the Thames, close to the riverbank. Old Father Thames had sheeted over completely, squeezing the hulls of ships in its frozen grip. St Katharine Docks sat opposite, beside the Tower of London itself. Almost home soil, Ben realized with relief. They were in Pickle Herring Street, and above them was the new bridge that daily continued to push its head above the London skyline.

"Tower Bridge," said Moon when Ben told him where they were. "The Uncreated One be praised."

"It's only a bridge," said Ben.

"Wrong again," said Moon, and he tousled the hair of the Hand of Heaven while he still had the chance.

Mickelwhite and Bedlam had almost ruined it all. They had raised the alarm too soon, and then gone rampaging on their own personal vendetta.

If you were tracking a beast to its lair, it was vital that

the creature didn't know it was being stalked. If Ben Kingdom hadn't brought the roof down on their stupid heads, Carter would have done it himself.

As it was, the explosion had worked in Carter's favour.

No doubt Ben and Moon thought that they escaped. What they didn't realize was that they had not only sealed their own doom but they had condemned the Watchers too. The ageing tunnel, which they had so clearly signposted as their route, only had one exit.

Carter smiled with sadistic glee; he knew exactly where they were headed and, if he responded quickly enough, he had time to prepare a welcoming party for them.

Jimmy Dips was hovering nearby, trying to ingratiate himself as usual, and Carter summoned him with a click of his fingers.

"Call out the heavy-battle brigades immediately," Carter ordered.

"What shall I tell them, sir?"

"Tell them to prepare for war!"

Ben had never felt so tired. All the emotion of the last few days had finally caught up with him and, far from Moon leaning on him for strength, it was Ben who found himself grateful for the old man's arm as they walked the last few steps to stand on the bridge.

Ben looked up at the two great towers. The bridge would be incredible when it was finished, Ben thought. For now it was a work in progress, scaffolding poles and girders surrounding the unfinished buildings and canvas tents crowning the towers, protecting the building work from the worst of the winter weather.

Wearily they started to cross, Ben concentrating on putting one foot in front of the other. To Ben's surprise, when they were almost halfway over Moon lifted his hand and waved. It was still the dark before the dawn and Ben had no idea who the old man was signalling to, until he saw the canvas lifting on the North Tower to reveal the glow of a lamp and a friendly face, followed by a rope ladder that rattled down to the ground.

Jago Moon smiled at Ben. "Home at last," he said.

Ben headed towards it, his spirits lifting with each step. It felt right to be joining the Watchers. He would see Nathaniel again! And together they could search for Pa and—

Then the screaming started.

Looking over his shoulder, Ben saw the Feathered Men as they exploded from the ground. They emerged from the Under like bats from a cave and shrieked as they took to the air. Ben counted three secret exits from the Under and watched in horror as the filthy creatures continued to swarm into the sky; carrion crows circling around a carcass.

They had been followed, Ben realized. He had led the Legion here.

From above his head came sounds of panic. The Feathered Men were ripping at the tent on the tower, tearing it away with their claws, leaving the Watchers exposed and vulnerable. A dozen more ladders unfurled, and Ben could see the adults helping the children over the side. A crossbow bolt whistled through the air and sank deeply into the surface of the bridge. Ben noticed that a thin rope was attached to it and more Watchers came whistling down, using it as a slip wire, hitting the ground running and ushering the young ones to safety north of the river in Tower Wharf and beyond.

It was not enough though. Ben could see Watchers, like knights on the battlements, striking at the fallen angels with quarterstaffs and swords, trying to fend them off.

And losing.

The Feathered Men were ferocious in their attack. They slashed at the Watchers with their talons, broke bones with their snapping beaks. A body fell past Ben, so close that he could see the horror in the man's eyes. Two

Feathered Men squabbled over another unfortunate Watcher, pulling him back and forth between them. Ben saw men being carried away into the air, hung beneath Feathered Men as helpless as rabbits in the claws of an eagle.

Then came the beating of another pair of wings, stronger and whiter than those of the Feathered Men. Ben's hopes rose as the Weeping Man launched himself into the air, his sword singing.

"Turn back, my brothers," the Weeping Man urged as the fallen angels flocked around him. "Go on in peace," he said, as his sword struck home. A severed wing spiralled to the ground, followed by a Feathered Man, plummeting until the ice of the Thames broke its fall. And its neck.

Ben realized that Jago Moon was no longer at his side. He could see him at the far side of the bridge already, shepherding the children to safety. But human Legionnaires had arrived now too and were closing the gap. Ben only hoped the Watchers had enough of a head start.

"Ben Kingdom!"

A voice rang out above the mayhem. Ben turned.

Claw Carter had found him and was calling him out.

He was standing on the low wall at the edge of the bridge below the North Tower. Carter was not alone, Ben could tell. He was holding another man prisoner, his hand clamped across the man's mouth and his claw hovering over the soft flesh of his oesophagus.

"Pa!" shouted Ben.

Claw Carter smiled maliciously. "A family reunion, how very touching."

"Don't you dare hurt him," challenged Ben.

"Or what?" said Carter.

Ben had no reply. He had never seen his father looking so battered and bruised. One eye was closed beneath a swelling the colour of old meat. His lip was fat and bloody, his clothes torn, his body limp.

"Hello, son," said Jonas Kingdom, his good eye winking.

"So," said Carter. "It's time for you to choose, Benjamin Kingdom. What's it to be? Join me in the Legion and become the Left Hand, the Son of the Sinister. Or follow poor, pathetic blind-eyed Moon, and become the Right Hand: the limp, weak leader of the losing side."

Carter ran his claw in a sawing motion across Jonas Kingdom's neck. "Don't let me influence you at all, Ben. You must do what your heart says. And if you choose the right-hand path and join the Watchers…well, you can always see your father again in Heaven."

Ben reached into his pocket.

"Let him go," he said.

He watched with satisfaction as Carter's eyes fixed on the small circle of metal he now held in his hand. "It's not really me you want, is it? It's this!"

"Give it to me!" Carter shouted.

"My Coin, my terms," said Ben. "I'll throw the Coin onto the ice where you can get your claw on it, and you let my father come to me."

Ben didn't have to wait for an answer, the expression of desperate need on Carter's face told him everything he needed to know. Coldly and casually Ben tossed the tiny disc over the side, to land on the frozen surface of the Thames.

But just at that instant, another of the Feathered Men dropped from the sky, its head hanging loose where the Weeping Man's sword had bitten deep. It hit the ice with a bone-shattering crunch. For a second nothing happened; then a spider's web of cracks splintered around it. The ice gave a mighty groan and split wide, as if the river had opened its mouth, sucking the Feathered Man and the Judas Coin down to the bottom of the Thames.

"You never do make the right choice, do you, boy?" snarled Carter, as he let his claw do its work, tracing a red line across Jonas Kingdom's throat.

Ben could only watch as his father's limp body followed the Coin over the edge and into the water.

CHAPTER 37

THE BATTLE OF TOWER BRIDGE

Ben didn't hesitate.

He jumped over the edge and followed his father.

He knew that the Thames could kill on the best of days. It was not the sort of water that you could drink. Every stinking slaughterhouse, every tannery, every factory on the banks of the river deposited their filth here. It was a toilet that ran through the heart of London; a place where rats swam and stray dogs went to die.

Ben held his breath tight inside his chest as he plunged beneath the surface of the freezing river. Would his first mouthful of the Thames be his last? Would it drag him to the bottom, never to return?

As soon as he was in the icy water, his body started to go into shock. The cold was so heavy that it was as if he was being squeezed in a vice. The blood in his ears was as loud as thunder.

So this is the end, thought Ben.

It was hard not to panic.

He looked around frantically, trying to find his father before the river claimed both their lives.

At first, he thought that Jonas had been swept away by the current, and his eyes searched the black waters with increasing desperation. He could hardly see his hand in front of his face and all the time he was drifting further away from the hole in the ice; further away from hope. Something heavy collided with his back and his heart lifted as he circled in the water, hoping to come face-to-face with his pa. Instead he found himself staring into the open maw of a Feathered Man. Shock surged through Ben's system and he nearly broke for the surface in fear until he saw the dead mirror of the fallen angel's eyes and the hideous angle of its broken neck.

It was another precious second lost. Time his father didn't have.

When Ben saw the blood, it was so black that he didn't recognize it at first. His eyes followed it, down, down. The trail led to the shape of a man, almost invisible in the darkness of the Thames; a motionless man, sinking out of sight.

Ben had no air left, but no choice either. He kicked down with both legs, pushing himself onwards. Ignoring the pain. Following the blood. After his pa.

When he finally reached him, there was nothing in his lungs except fire.

He put his right arm around his father, feeling the same rush of strength he had experienced when he rescued Mr. Smutts. Then he searched for the hole in the ice that was the only way back to the light.

I won't let you die, Pa.

Ben kicked and thrashed and dragged himself through the water.

I can't let you leave me.

Closer towards the jagged window in the ice.

Please don't leave me like Mum did.

Up. Up…

And out.

Gasping, exhausted, Ben hauled himself back onto the creaking ice and dragged his father after him.

Jonas Kingdom wasn't moving.

His lips were blue. His chest was motionless. The blood had ceased to pump from his wound.

Overhead, the Feathered Men were still screaming. In

spite of his skill with a sword, the Weeping Man was overwhelmed. They dived at him, ripping at his wings with their talons. Ben saw his feathers torn out in chunks, the stripes of claws on his face, his chest, his arms. Still more Feathered Men swooped in, shrieking with insane pleasure as they pecked and slashed.

Above Ben on the bridge, Claw Carter was laughing.

Benjamin felt the anger swelling within him. The trembling in his hands. The burning inside. The mounting pressure of unearthly power waiting to be released.

I'm going to make you pay for this!

He rolled his left hand into a fist. A tight ball of fury that felt so good. He would smash the smile from Carter's face. He would kill Mickelwhite. Destroy the Legion. Kill them all. He would make them pay. He would, he would…

And then he let his fury go, as a supernatural calm fell upon him.

He studied his right hand as if it was the first time he had ever seen it. Suddenly he knew what he had to do.

Ben raised his right hand tentatively, elevating his arm until it was high above his head. The stabbing sensation of hot needles had never been more intense and Ben had to clench his teeth against it, but as he rode the wave of agony, it seemed to reach a crescendo at a level he could stand. Just.

An instinct somewhere deep inside seemed to guide him. He breathed slowly through the pain, calmed his thoughts and responded, letting himself become... whatever it was that Jago Moon had been rambling on about.

Ben made a mental note to pay more attention the next time Moon was explaining what was happening to his life; of course, that was assuming he even got out of this alive. The flow of energy began to falter as Ben became distracted and inner peace was replaced by panic. *I don't know what to do!* Ben screamed inside. He wriggled his fingers, clenched his fist, his movements becoming increasingly frantic.

Nothing happened.

The realization hit him like a fist in his gut. All along the length of the bridge, he could hear the shouts and screams of the Watchers; and there wasn't a damned thing that he could do about it.

He was helpless, Ben knew that. Everyone was expecting him to be this great leader, but what was he really? A kid from the wrong end of Old Gravel Lane.

Ben flinched as another scream tore the air.

All that he wanted was for this to be over. No more Feathered Men, no more Legion. No more street kids getting hurt.

Stop.

Somewhere a small girl was crying in fear. She reminded him of Molly.

Stop.

The Feathered Men caught hold of another Watcher and tore at him with their beaks. Ben had to turn his eyes away from the hurting, the fighting, the blood.

Please make it stop!

His right hand began to tremble again, as if the pricking of his conscience were somehow linked to the needle-jab sensation. Hesitantly, he rolled his fingers into a ball and lifted his arm above his head once more. This time the power did not fade.

And the clouds responded.

Ben held his right fist aloft and felt the awesome power throbbing with renewed force. The great and powerful Right Hand of Heaven, that was what Moon had said Ben could be. But Moon had it wrong, Ben realized; this force wasn't his own to wield. The Hand was just a channel. He was a conduit for something much greater than he or Jago Moon could ever imagine; the raw energy at the heart of the universe. Ben didn't know what that source was and he certainly didn't understand how it could work through him, but one thing he did know: it was time for the fighting to end.

Ben extended a finger and the clouds blossomed in submission.

Ben saw Carter.

I choose not to hate you.

The clouds grew as dark and deep as the ocean and then began to fill with other-wordly fire; flames that swirled and danced in the sky.

Ben swept his right hand upwards, and the clouds became a pillar, stretching up further than the eye could see. He saw his father's prone body.

I choose not to be filled with bitterness.

Slowly Ben lowered his hand, allowing his actions to be guided by intuition, not his own thoughts. In a final graceful gesture, he closed his fingers slowly and pulled his right hand in towards his chest.

And in answer, the clouds gave up their load.

The first hailstone hit the ground two inches from Carter's foot. It was the size of a musket ball and twice as hard. The second one struck Carter on the shoulder. The third on his head.

Carter screamed in pain, trying to shield himself from the torrent of ice.

In the skies, the hailstones whistled as they sought out their targets. Ben saw wings pierced and the Feathered Men spinning helplessly as the power of flight was taken from them. They fell onto the bridge, onto the groaning ice, staggering in confusion and distress as the missiles shattered all around them. Not dead, but defeated, Ben understood. Overwhelmed by the white rain that sought out the Legion but left the Watchers untouched.

Ben's ears were filled with the hammering of falling hail and the moaning of the Legion as they ran away, escaping into the Under.

When Ben looked again, Carter had gone too. Another rat scurrying back into his hole.

I really hate rats, Ben thought.

The clouds lifted. The onslaught ceased.

On the bridge, the Watchers were cheering as they continued to evacuate the last of the stragglers. Scattered all around, the wounded were groaning and the Watchers were tending to all of them, friend and foe alike. Life would go on.

But not for everyone.

Ben let his own eyes drop to his feet, to rest on Jonas Kingdom, motionless on the ice. He collapsed to his knees beside his father's body. Blue with cold. Red with blood.

It was Christmas Day, Ben thought; the same day that he had lost his mother.

Ben didn't know how long he sat there on the frozen Thames. He was shivering uncontrollably in his sodden clothes, but he couldn't find the strength to move.

Jonas Kingdom hadn't moved either since Ben had pulled him from the water.

Ben was vaguely aware that he was not alone on the ice and he looked up to see Nathaniel and the Weeping Man standing beside him. They both looked drained to their very core. Tears painted all their faces.

"It's not over, Benjamin Kingdom," said the Weeping Man.

"Haven't I done enough for the Watchers today?" spat Ben. "What more do you want from me?"

"Place your right hand on your father's chest."

"And then what?"

"You are the Right Hand of Heaven," said the Weeping Man. "You tell me."

CHAPTER 38

THE HAND

Ben placed his right hand on his father's chest and let the power flow from his fingers.

Jonas Kingdom remained colder than a stone.

Please, thought Ben, urging his father to respond.

Ben repositioned his hand, feeling the throbbing inside his own skin, but seeing no response from Jonas.

Please.

His father's lips were the grey of dead fish.

Ben looked pleadingly at the Weeping Man and the angel gently placed his own hand on top of Ben's.

Please!

His father's eyes held no spark of life.

His father's chest was still. His skin was cold.

His father's heart was...stirring faintly inside his ribcage, as frail as a newborn bird.

The merest hint of pink touched his father's cheeks. His eyelids fluttered. Once. Twice.

Bracing himself for the worst, Ben ripped open what remained of his father's shirt collar to see the jagged tear left by Carter's claw and saw the wound knit itself together, the flesh made whole again. The chest below the scar began to rise. The heart within beat stronger.

Then, with a start, Jonas sat up and looked around him, dazed, like a man who had been asleep a thousand years and didn't recognize the world.

"Hello, Pa," said Ben, as their eyes met.

Jonas embraced him then as he had never done before, fiercely and tightly. Ben felt that his own bones might break, but that was fine by him. At least he would die happy.

"I was so worried about you, Ben," said Jonas, blinking back tears. "I thought I'd lost you, son." Jonas held Ben's face in both hands so that he could drink him in more deeply.

"I love you, Benjamin," said Jonas Kingdom at last.

"I know, Pa," said Ben.

And with nothing else to be said, they picked themselves

up off the ice and set off to find the other Watchers. The three Kingdom men and their friend, the Weeping Man.

As they slowly walked away, Ben noticed that his head felt naked and he realized that he had lost his billycock somewhere. *I really loved that hat,* he thought wistfully.

A lopsided grin spread right across his face as he remembered the hail that he had brought from the sky, and the expression on Carter's face when the stones had started cracking him on the head. Ben wiggled his fingers experimentally and wondered what else they could do.

Although his body was absolutely freezing, he felt warm on the inside like he never had before. And he felt proud of the choice that he had made, to be the Right Hand, not the Left.

The boy done good, he thought contentedly.

And he was especially pleased that he had outwitted Claw Carter.

He tapped his pocket just to check. Still there.

It wasn't the real Coin that he had thrown into the Thames, of course. He had tricked them all. It was the mouldy old farthing that he'd had all the time.

Ben smiled.

Ain't life grand.

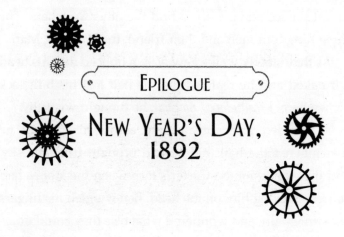

Scars were good, in Claw Carter's opinion. They reminded you of mistakes not to be made again. Defeat was good too, because it sharpened a man's desire to win the next bout.

If the Coin had been denied him, then he needed a new weapon and he knew where to look to find one. Carter had not left the Dark Library for days. He couldn't remember when he had last eaten, although he knew that Ruby Johnson was at his beck and call, bringing him sandwiches of rare and bloody beef.

He turned a dry page that had lain ignored for decades. *Upon the summoning of the Nightmare Child,* he read.

Happy New Year, Benjamin Kingdom. Enjoy it while you may.

GET READY FOR BEN'S NEXT BATTLE!

THE BATTLES OF BEN KINGDOM
THE FEAST OF RAVENS

Ben gazed up at the Tower of London and shuddered. It was a cold monument with a dark and bloodstained history and he was afraid that the Legion were about to write their own gruesome chapter. The crown jewels were no longer here; they were gone along with the Queen and the entire company of yeoman wardens. Only the ravens had remained, joined by hundreds of Legionnaires gathered for the Feast. Mr Sweet's voice echoed across the courtyard and Ben listened in silence, his hands tied behind his back and a big fat guard at his side. He was a prisoner, awaiting his fate...

OUT SEPTEMBER 2013

ISBN: 9781409546245

EPUB: 9781409557357 KINDLE: 9781409557364

BEN'S GUIDE
TO LONDON SLANG

An unorthodox glossary for some of the
more unusual words to be found in this book.

ballast heaver: big blokes paid to lift very heavy goods (ballast), into the holds of ships to improve stability.

billycock: a felt hat with a low, rounded crown, like a bowler. The best sort of hat there is.

bobby: a police officer, named after Robert "Bobby" Peel, founder of the Metropolitan Police in 1829.

brougham carriage: a light, four-wheeled horse-drawn carriage. The footplate provides an excellent free ride for those who are light of foot and empty of pocket, like me.

bullseye lantern: oil-fuelled, usually handheld, lantern with a round glass face like a bullseye (great for skulking).

chancer: a con man or crafty opportunist.

coal-whipper: someone who unloads coal out of the hold of a ship. A very mucky business indeed.

cooper: a maker or repairer of barrels and casks.

lascar: a sailor or militiaman from India, Burma, Ceylon and other lands, now employed on European ships.

his nibs: what we call stuck-up toffs who think they're more intelligent and more important than they really are.

monkeyshines: mischievous or playful tricks – good stuff!

mudlark: someone, usually an underappreciated boy, who makes a living scavenging in river mud for items of value. It does mean you get to keep the richest pickings for yourself though.

privy: outdoor loo/bog, usually located in a small shed away from the main living quarters (because they stink!).

road-apple: a big steaming dollop of horse manure. Recommended as a makeshift (but messy) weapon in emergencies.

rookery: an overcrowded, under-sanitised city slum. Your home, if you are poor and unlucky. Rookeries have nicked their name from the nesting habits of rooks, great crow-like birds who live crammed into noisy colonies in the treetops.

snuff it: to die, kick the bucket, give up the ghost, etc. It happens a lot in Victorian London, hence why we have so many ways of saying it.

skylark: to mess about, play tricks and have a good time.

tosher: a filthy type who makes a living scavenging in the sewers. Easily identified by their stench.

P. S. *Toshers' dogs are even dirtier than their owners.*

Acknowledgements

Writing this book has been a pleasure from start to finish and I have been supported, guided and loved by some wonderful people every step of the way.

Special thanks go to Gideon McCubbine... if you hadn't been in my class I might never have met your mum, the talented and generous editor, Helen Greathead. Thank you, Helen, for the hours you kindly spent editing your son's teacher's homework. Thank you too, for introducing me to my agent, the marvellous Anne Finnis. Thank you, Anne, for everything that you have done to help my lifelong dream come true. Thanks also to the incredible Caroline Hill-Trevor, for taking Ben's battles to lands near and far. This is where the adventure starts!

One glance at the beautiful cover of this book is testament to the skill and love that many talented people have poured into it. My thanks go out to Rebecca Hill for finding a home for Ben Kingdom with Usborne, Hannah Cobley for her outstanding cover design, and my cover artist and illustrator, David Wyatt, for bringing the world of the Watchers to such vivid life. Special thanks also to my editor, Stephanie King. Stephanie, you have been Ben's first champion; your insight and enthusiasm have made this book better than I could have ever managed on my own. *Thank you all.*

I'm a family man and so I have to end by thanking the people who fill my life with joy. Mum and Dad, this book would not have been possible without you; I owe you so much. Amanda, you always knew I'd make it one day; I haven't forgotten. Mum and Jack, thank you for cheering me on. Ben and Lucy, being your dad is the proudest achievement of my life; you make me smile every day. My darling Julie, I don't have enough words to say how much I love you. And to the one who set me on this path all those years ago. *I love you all.*

About the Author

ANDREW BEASLEY was born in Hertfordshire, and has spent most of his life with his nose buried in a book.

As a student he read law in Bristol, but was disappointed to discover that life as a lawyer wasn't as exciting as books had led him to believe. He then spent a number of years travelling extensively across Europe for work, although he didn't see much of it because he was usually reading a book.

Andrew is now a primary school teacher, where he shares his passion for storytelling with his class. Andrew lives in Cornwall with his wife and their two children, Ben and Lucy. *The Claws of Evil* is his debut novel.

THE BATTLES CONTINUE AT
WWW.BENKINGDOM.COM